FROM THE
NANCY DREW FILES

THE CASE: Nancy tries to track down an industrial spy at Jetstream Aviation—and prove the innocence of a young test pilot.

CONTACT: George's new boyfriend, Gary Powell, has been accused of selling the plans for a secret new airplane to a rival company in France.

SUSPECTS: Sasha Petrov—the irresistible Soviet dancer has taken a deep interest in Nancy and in her investigation.

Dmitri Kolchak—Sasha's official chaperon and a former pilot in the Soviet air force, he's determined to keep Nancy away from Sasha and from the case.

Bill Fairgate—Jetstream's designer thinks he isn't being paid enough. Is he now secretly working for the rival French company?

Yves Goulard—the dancers' pianist has expressed a desire to return to France and retire—at the age of thirty.

COMPLICATIONS: Nancy's drawn to Sasha—but what if he's the spy? And what about her boyfriend, Ned?

Books in The Nancy Drew Files ™ Series

Available from ARCHWAY Paperbacks

THE
NANCY DREW
FILES™

A Summer of Love Trilogy #1

Case 48
A DATE WITH DECEPTION

CAROLYN KEENE

AN ARCHWAY PAPERBACK
Published by POCKET BOOKS
New York   London   Toronto   Sydney   Tokyo   Singapore

AN ARCHWAY PAPERBACK *Original*

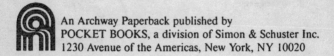

An Archway Paperback published by
POCKET BOOKS, a division of Simon & Schuster Inc.
1230 Avenue of the Americas, New York, NY 10020

ISBN: 0-671-67500-1

First Archway Paperback printing June 1990

10 9 8 7 6 5 4 3 2 1

A DATE WITH
DECEPTION

Chapter

One

"Т HIS IS ABSOLUTE PARADISE," Bess Marvin said dreamily. "I just might spend the rest of my life right here, taking in all this scenery."

Nancy Drew shook her reddish gold hair out of her eyes and looked at the foamy waves rolling up on the white, sandy beach. "It's definitely gorgeous," she agreed.

"Bess doesn't mean the natural scenery, Nancy." George Fayne glanced at her cousin Bess and grinned. "She's talking about the human kind. The male, human kind."

Bess's blue eyes sparkled as she looked at all the guys on the beach, sunbathing, swimming, and playing volleyball. "I'm talking about

THE NANCY DREW FILES

both," she said, rubbing some sunscreen on her shoulders. "Both kinds of scenery are just about perfect. And so is this vacation. I'm so glad your aunt invited us to come here, Nancy."

Nancy's aunt Eloise, who usually spent her summers at her house in New York's Adirondack Mountains, had decided to exchange houses with someone from the Hamptons, a group of small oceanside villages on the eastern end of Long Island, in New York. When she'd invited Nancy and her two best friends to spend their vacation with her, the girls had jumped at the chance: days of sunning and swimming, nights of eating at great seafood restaurants or dancing at small clubs. As Bess said, it was just about perfect.

"Well," George said, getting up from her beach towel and pushing her short, dark hair behind her ears, "I think I'll get wet again. See you in a few minutes!" Long legged and athletic, George sprinted across the sand and plunged into the gray-blue waters of the Atlantic Ocean.

Watching her, Bess smiled. "George sure is happy these days."

"I know," Nancy agreed. "It's nice, isn't it? Gary seems like a great guy."

George had met Gary Powell during a volleyball game two weeks earlier, and the two of them had hit it off immediately. Twenty years old, Gary lived in the Hamptons and had been hired as a test pilot for Jetstream, Inc., a local company that designed and built jet planes.

"She's so lucky." Bess sighed. She pulled a brush out of her pink canvas beach bag and tugged it through her long blond hair. Next she took out a small mirror. "I have to admit I'm jealous," she said, eyeing her slightly sun-burned nose. "I mean, George has Gary. And you've got Ned—even though he isn't here."

Ned Nickerson, Nancy's longtime boy-friend, was working at a summer job back in their hometown, River Heights. Nancy was hoping he'd be able to come east to visit them. Even though she missed him, she was still having a great time, and she knew Bess was, too.

"Come on, Bess," she said, her blue eyes alight with laughter. "You've been out with at least five different guys since we got here!"

"I know, and it's been fun," Bess agreed. "But I'm not just talking about dating. I'm talking about romance."

Still laughing, Nancy stood up and shook the sand from her blue- and white-striped towel. Bess was always looking for romance. "Well," Nancy said teasingly, "maybe Sasha Petrov will dance away with your heart."

Bess smiled. "I've already thought of that."

Sasha Petrov was a young ballet dancer, a rising star in his own country, the Soviet Union, although he wasn't very well known elsewhere. He was coming to the United States for the summer to join an international ballet institute sponsored by the Hamptons Cultural Society—talented young dancers from all over the world were taking part in it.

Nancy's aunt Eloise, who was on the board of directors of the Cultural Society, was Sasha's official sponsor, and she'd asked the three girls to help entertain him when he wasn't busy rehearsing.

"I wonder what he looks like," Bess said now.

"What who looks like?" George asked as she rejoined them.

"Sasha Petrov," Nancy said. "Bess decided that the best way to entertain him will be with a little romance."

"I should have known!" Laughing, George toweled off and pulled on an oversize yellow T-shirt. "I guess we'd better get going," she said to Bess. "Sasha's plane gets here at two, and that gives you only two hours to get ready."

"Right," Bess agreed with a grin. "After all, I don't want to greet him with sand in my hair. It wouldn't be good for international relations!"

At one-fifteen that afternoon Nancy pulled her rented Honda into the parking lot of the small Hamptons airport. She, George, and Bess got out to wait for Eloise, who pulled her car up next to theirs.

Tall and elegant, Eloise Drew got out and smoothed down her shining brown hair. "I'm so glad the weather is cooperating," she said. "It couldn't be a more perfect day." She smiled warmly at the girls, who were wearing brightly colored cotton sundresses. "You three certainly look nice. I think this is the first time all summer that I haven't seen you in bathing suits and flip-flops—during the day, at any rate."

"First impressions are important," Bess said seriously.

George gave her a playful punch on the arm. "She means important for Sasha Petrov."

Eloise laughed. "Well, good luck, Bess!"

"See?" Bess said. "She doesn't think I'm crazy."

"We don't either, Bess," Nancy said as they walked into the small terminal. "We just think you should meet the guy before you decide to fall in love with him."

Across the room a small crowd had gathered to wait for the arrival of the Soviets. Several other members of the cultural committee were there as well as Dana Harding, the dance institute's artistic director. Slender and intense, Dana was nervously tapping her foot. When she spotted Eloise, she waved her over.

"Oh, dear, Dana's looking very edgy," Eloise commented. "I can't blame her, though. She organized this entire project, and she's very anxious for it to succeed. I'll go wait with

5

her," she added. "Meet you outside when the plane comes in."

For a little while longer, the group milled around, chatting and laughing. Then the drone of an airplane was heard, and everyone moved quickly for the doors.

The airport was so small that passengers simply got off the plane and walked across the runway to the terminal.

"This is so exciting!" Bess said as they gathered outside. "I just hope this wind doesn't wreck my hair," she added, holding it down with both hands.

"There it is!" George cried.

With the sunlight glinting off its silver-tipped wings, the small charter jet circled the airport, then landed smoothly on the runway.

In a few minutes the plane taxied toward the terminal. The ground crew hurried out and wheeled some portable steps into place. Then the door opened and a tall, bulky man with a head of thick gray hair appeared and started down the steps.

"Too old and too big," Bess said immediately. "He can't be Sasha."

"It's not," said Eloise, who'd joined them. "I believe that's Dmitri Kolchak. He's the Soviet chaperon. Ah!" she said, gesturing toward the plane, "that must be Marina."

Marina Zukova, Sasha's dance partner, was slender and beautiful, with gleaming black hair that fell to her shoulders in a mass of waves. Moving gracefully, she joined Dmitri Kolchak at the bottom of the steps.

"Uh-oh," Bess murmured, "if she's around, I don't know if I'll stand a chance with Sasha."

"I wouldn't worry too much," Eloise told her, smiling. "From what I've heard, I gather Marina's relationship with Sasha is strictly professional."

"That's a relief," Bess responded.

Just then a smiling young man burst through the door, gave a cheerful wave to the waiting group, and trotted quickly down to the runway.

"That has to be Sasha," Bess announced excitedly. "He's gorgeous!"

Nancy and George couldn't argue with her. Sasha Petrov was extremely good-looking. Of medium height, he had a dancer's build, lean but muscular. His face was slender, with high cheekbones and large, heavy-lidded eyes. As he walked toward Dana Harding, he pushed his golden brown hair off his forehead and gave her a charming grin. Eloise walked over with her arm extended to greet Sasha.

It was a few minutes before Eloise was able to introduce Sasha to the girls, so Bess had time to comb her hair and check her face to make sure a big blob of dirt hadn't suddenly appeared on it.

Finally Eloise brought Sasha over to them,

introducing him to George first and then to Bess, who was instantly captivated by his smile.

"And this is my niece, Nancy Drew," Eloise said.

"Hello," Nancy said, shaking his hand. "Welcome to the United States."

"It's a great pleasure to be here." Sasha squeezed Nancy's hand, his eyes gleaming with admiration. They were an incredibly clear shade of sky blue, Nancy noted.

"Nancy and her friends are spending their vacation with me," Eloise told Sasha. "Whenever you have any free time from your rehearsals and classes, they've offered to show you and Marina around."

"How lucky for me," Sasha said, looking at Nancy and still holding on to her hand. He gave her a wide-eyed, innocent grin. "I think my stay here is going to be even better than I imagined."

Nancy finally managed to free her hand, but she couldn't help smiling. Sasha, she decided, was really cute. He was also quite a flirt. Too bad she couldn't just come right out and tell him to flirt with Bess instead of her. Maybe she could drop a hint later.

"I hope you like the ocean," she told him. "The beaches here are really beautiful."

"I'm sure they are," he said. "But I have the feeling I won't be looking at the view too much. I would rather be looking at you."

To her surprise, Nancy felt an agreeable warmth sweep through her. Usually such blatant flirting annoyed her, but coming from Sasha it was somehow charming. Maybe it was his guileless blue eyes.

"Well, anyway, you probably won't have much time for going to the beach with me. Me *and* my friends," Nancy reminded him with a grin.

"Of course. Your two charming friends," Sasha agreed, then promptly steered the conversation back to flirting. "Tell me, do you believe in love at first sight?"

Shaking her head in amusement, Nancy glanced to her right, hoping to bring George and Bess into the conversation. They'd gotten separated from her by Dmitri Kolchak and Marina Zukova, who were openly staring at her and Sasha now. Their faces had the same expression: complete disapproval.

Uh-oh, Nancy thought. They obviously don't like what they're seeing. I just hope they don't think I'm the one who's doing the flirting.

She decided to get Sasha to talk with somebody else. He was handsome, and it was fun being flirted with, but she didn't want him or anybody else to think she was taking it seriously.

Nancy spotted her aunt Eloise and was just about to call out to her when Dana Harding shouted, "I think that plane's in trouble!"

The pleasant chatter stopped, and in dead silence everyone looked up where Dana was pointing. A small white jet was just approaching the airport, and from the way its body was wobbling, Nancy guessed the pilot was fighting to keep the nose of the plane up.

As the plane passed overhead, its nose did dip sharply. Then suddenly it fell into a spin, its sleek body twisting and turning, heading straight for the crowd.

Chapter

Two

THAT PLANE is going to crash into us! Nancy decided, joining everyone in a flat-out run for the terminal. Sasha gripped her arm, and she knew he was as alarmed as she was. Even as she ran, Nancy couldn't take her eyes off the plane spiraling closer and closer to the ground.

Then, at the last possible moment, the pilot managed to pull the nose up. The plane roared over the runway, whipping the air into a minihurricane.

Siren blaring, a fire truck sped out toward the end of the runway. The plane was looping back for an emergency landing.

11

Nancy held her breath as the plane came in low. It hit the runway, bounced off, bumped again, then tilted to the side, spinning completely around before coming to a stop.

The truck was ready, and everyone watched breathlessly as the ground crew rushed toward the plane with hoses.

"Come on!" someone murmured tensely. "Get that pilot out of there before the thing explodes!"

The pilot's door was already open, and in seconds a tall, lanky figure emerged and leaped to the ground.

"Oh, no!" George cried. "It's Gary!" Her dark eyes wide with fright, she pushed her way to the edge of the onlookers and ran toward the plane.

Gary caught sight of her and waved to let her know he was all right. George stopped where she was, her tall figure relaxing a bit.

Still standing close to Nancy, Sasha said, "This Gary. He is your friend's brother?"

"Her boyfriend," Nancy said, her eyes still on the plane. She'd only just noticed the bold blue Jetstream logo on its tail. She waited tensely to see what would happen.

The ground crew was still aiming a hose at the plane, but Gary and his mechanic were standing casually close to the plane. At one point the mechanic even threw back his head and laughed, then patted Gary on the back.

Nancy breathed a sigh of relief. Gary was all

right, and it looked as if the plane wasn't going to blow up, either.

Gary turned and waved again to George. Then he trotted over to her, put his arms around her, and swung her off her feet in a big bear hug.

A cheer went up from the onlookers, and Nancy joined in, smiling at Sasha. That's when she noticed that he still had hold of her arm.

When he saw her notice, Sasha let go of it. Reluctantly, it seemed to Nancy.

"Such a frightening experience," he said. "And that hug—they are in love?"

Nancy nodded. "I think they might be," she told Sasha.

"That is good." Sasha took her hand in his, smiling that disarming smile once again. "I have never been in love myself—not yet. I have never had time for it. But I have the feeling I might like it."

"Well, I guess we know who waltzed away with Sasha's heart," Bess said that evening. She looked at Nancy and grinned. "And it sure wasn't me. Right, Nan?"

Nancy shook her head. "It wasn't me, either, Bess. I think Sasha just likes to flirt."

The three girls were in their room, getting ready for the reception Eloise was holding for all the dancers that night at her house. The guest room was large and airy, with sliding screen doors leading out onto a wooden deck.

13

The low and rhythmic roar of waves rolling onto the beach was soothing, drifting into the room through the screens.

"Today he decided to flirt with me," Nancy went on, pulling a pair of loose white cotton pants out of the closet. "Tonight it'll probably be you."

"Maybe," Bess said doubtfully. "But from the way he was looking at you, I got the feeling it was pretty serious flirting. Didn't you think so, George?"

"I don't know," George said, drying her just-washed hair with a fluffy blue towel. "Sorry, Bess, but Gary's landing kind of pushed everything else out of my mind." She gave a little shudder. "I just couldn't believe it when I saw him climbing out of the plane. Did I tell you that apparently a huge downdraft hit the nose and forced the plane into a dive? Gary could easily have been killed."

"But he wasn't," Nancy said. "And after that landing, he's practically a hero."

George smiled. "I know. Jetstream's really proud of him for saving their plane. Gary said he was just glad it wasn't the new one."

"What new one?" Bess asked, rummaging in a drawer of the wicker chest for a pair of panty hose.

"Jetstream's come up with some special new plane they're really excited about," George said. "It's called the Jetstar. Gary tested it a couple of times, and the engineers and designers are making some changes now. They're keeping all the plans under tight security because they don't want the competition to find out about it. It's supposed to knock everybody's socks off."

"Speaking of knocking somebody's socks off," Bess said, "how will this do?" She held up a gauzy, peach-colored dress and fluffed out the short skirt.

"It'll look fabulous," Nancy told her, buttoning the cuffs on her silky yellow blouse.

"But will it get a certain dancer's attention?"

"It'll get *everybody's* attention," George said dryly.

"You know who I mean," Bess said.

Laughing, Nancy tossed a flowered pillow at her friend. "If Sasha Petrov doesn't notice you tonight, Bess, then he ought to have his beautiful blue eyes examined. I'll see you two later— I'm going to see if Aunt Eloise needs any help."

Nancy hurried downstairs and glanced around the living room with approval before heading for the kitchen. The house was perfect for a large party. The main floor had high ceilings and large rooms that opened into one another and onto wide decks outside.

By eight o'clock that night, the house was filled with the sound of music, the good smells of food, and the chatter and laughter of at least fifty people.

"Keep me away from the buffet table," Bess

groaned, eyeing the enormous platters of cold shrimp, bowls of pasta salad, and crusty loaves of French bread. "I can feel myself gaining weight just looking at it."

"I can hear my stomach growling just looking at it," Nancy said. She picked up two plates and handed one to Bess. "Come on, Bess, you're the only one in the world who thinks you need to lose five pounds."

"Well, all right." Bess took the plate and sighed. "I wouldn't be able to hold out, anyway. I can always swim it off."

"That'll be the day!" Shaking her head in amusement, Nancy reached for the bread. Another hand got there first, though, and glancing up, Nancy saw Sasha Petrov smiling at her.

"Nancy." He was dressed casually, in pleated cotton slacks and a loose blue polo shirt that matched the color of his eyes. "When I heard this reception was being held at your aunt's house, I couldn't wait to get here."

Nancy decided to deliberately misunderstand him. "I don't blame you," she said. "The food looks great, doesn't it?"

"Great, yes," he agreed, still looking at her. "But the company is even better."

Suddenly Nancy saw Bess watching them, an I-told-you-so expression on her face. "Sasha," she said quickly, "you remember my friend Bess Marvin, don't you?"

Giving Nancy a look that told her he knew

she was up to something, Sasha turned to Bess. "Of course I remember. You look—what is the word? Fabulous?"

"Thank you," Bess said with a blush. "Fabulous is more than I hoped for." She gave Sasha the salad forks and a big smile. "So, how do you like the house where you and Marina and Dmitri are staying? It's in the village, isn't it?" He nodded. "Is it comfortable?"

"Very comfortable," Sasha said. "And I can bicycle to the institute every day."

Without saying anything, Nancy slipped away, leaving Sasha to Bess. Carrying her plate into the living area, she noticed that George, Gary, and her aunt Eloise were standing with a plump, middle-aged woman with graying brown hair. Her aunt caught her eye and waved Nancy over.

"Nancy, here's someone I want you to meet," Eloise said, turning to the woman. "This is Eileen Martin. Eileen's the secretary of the Cultural Society. She's been very friendly to me since I arrived in the Hamptons. Eileen, this is my niece, Nancy Drew. She's my brother Carson's daughter."

"Nancy, I'm so glad to meet you," Eileen said warmly, shaking Nancy's hand. Her brown eyes were unexpectedly shrewd. "I understand you were at the airport earlier today—I guess you witnessed Gary's incredible landing."

"I sure did," Nancy said. "It was amazing,

17

but I hope I don't see another one like it for a long time."

Tall, sandy-haired Gary grinned at her. "I hope I don't, either," he admitted. "Eileen's a senior engineer at Jetstream," he explained to Nancy.

"Now," Eileen said, patting him on the hand. "You come with me. I'm going to fill your plate, Mr. Powell. You need to put on some weight."

Without waiting for an answer, Eileen led Gary off to the buffet table. George rolled her eyes and followed them.

Eloise smiled fondly. "Eileen mothers all the young men at Jetstream," she told Nancy. Then she lowered her voice. "Her own son was only twenty-one when he died in an accident two years ago, and I'm sure that's the reason she's a bit of a mother hen."

Nancy was about to ask what kind of accident when Eloise excused herself to greet some new arrivals.

Left alone for the moment Nancy wandered through the rooms, meeting the dancers and listening to their conversations. After a while she decided to get some fresh air and carried a plate and a glass of cider out onto one of the decks.

The lulling sound of the ocean was strong out there. Nancy set her plate and glass down on a table and walked over to lean against the

"Nancy," Sasha said, and moved closer.

Oh, no, she thought. He wants to kiss me. Tell him now and get it over with.

Sasha reached out for her, and Nancy held *her* hand up to stop him. Just as their fingers touched, a long dark shadow fell over them.

Chapter

Three

STARTLED, NANCY JUMPED AWAY from Sasha and whirled around to face the house. Framed in the doorway was Dmitri Kolchak, his thick, gray eyebrows pulled together in a scowl.

"Sasha," the Soviet chaperon said, "I have been searching for you." Then he spoke a few phrases in Russian.

Nancy didn't understand a word, but she got the idea. Dmitri didn't like the cozy scene he thought he had interrupted between her and Sasha. From the way he kept glancing at her, Nancy believed he thought she was the one who was pursuing Sasha.

Sasha laughed and held up his hand. "All

right, Dmitri, all right." He turned to Nancy and grinned. "Dmitri is worried that I'm monopolizing you and keeping you from the other guests."

I'll bet, Nancy thought wryly. But she smiled at Dmitri, anyway. "Sasha's the one who should be circulating more," she told him. "After all, the party's partly in his honor."

"A very good point, Miss Drew." Stepping to one side, Dmitri gestured politely for her and Sasha to go back in to join the crowd.

"You must forgive Dmitri," Sasha whispered to Nancy as the three of them went inside. He waited until the chaperon walked over to talk to Marina, and then continued. "His job is to look after Marina and me, and he takes his work very seriously."

"I don't blame him," Nancy said. Actually, she was glad Dmitri had come along. She hadn't been too crazy about that cozy scene, either. She still had to set Sasha straight, but this wasn't the right moment. "Has he been with you a long time?" she asked.

"Two years," Sasha told her. "Before this, he was a pilot in our air force."

"Now he's a chaperon? He just travels with you from place to place to make sure you stay out of trouble? That's a big switch, isn't it?"

"Yes. My government gave him the job because he knows a lot of languages," Sasha explained. "Anyway, you know the military—very strict about following orders. Dmitri is good at that."

He glanced over at his dance partner, who was prowling the crowded room restlessly. "So is Marina. All she wants to do is rehearse, day and night. No time for anything else. She gives Dmitri no trouble." Sasha laughed. "But I'm afraid I give him a big headache. He thinks because I want to have a good time, I will neglect my dancing and be a disgrace to my country."

"Well, I sure wouldn't want you to do that," Nancy said. Smiling, she excused herself and walked over to George and Gary, who were at the front door. "You guys aren't leaving, are you?" she asked.

"We're going to take a walk on the beach," George said, carrying her leather sandals. "I'll be back, but Gary won't. He has to go."

"I've got a meeting early in the morning," Gary explained, rolling up the cuffs of his slacks. "I don't know what it's about, but I was told it's important."

"Maybe it's about the new plane," George said. "It might be ready for you to take up again."

"I don't think so," Gary said doubtfully. "Eileen didn't say anything about it tonight." With a grin, he lowered his voice and spoke very mysteriously. "Of course, we're not supposed to discuss it at all. Who knows? The competition might have sent a spy here tonight—disguised as a ballet dancer."

Nancy laughed. "Maybe they just want to give you a commendation for that landing today."

"I bet Nancy's right," George put in, affectionately looping her arm through her boyfriend's. Her dark eyes glowed with pride. "You're the best flyer they have. They're probably going to give you a plaque."

"The best award would be more time in the sky," Gary said, his voice enthusiastic as it always was when he talked of flying. "Well, anyway, I'll find out tomorrow. Night, Nancy."

After George and Gary left, Nancy went back to the buffet table and helped herself to some fresh fruit and cookies. As she moved away, she saw Bess standing near the fireplace, talking with a man Nancy hadn't met. He was about thirty, she guessed, dark haired and extremely handsome.

Trust Bess to find one of the best-looking guys here tonight, she thought with a smile. Even if he is a little old.

In a few minutes the man bent low over Bess's hand and touched his lips to it. Then he moved away to talk with Dmitri Kolchak, and Nancy walked over to Bess.

"Who was that?" she asked.

Bess sighed. "He kissed my hand," she murmured dreamily.

"I noticed," Nancy said. "Does he have a name?"

"Yves Goulard," Bess said, sighing again. "He's French. Isn't he gorgeous?"

"Mmm. Is he a dancer?"

"No, a pianist. He's the accompanist for the dance institute." Bess gave herself a shake, her blue eyes sparkling with excitement. "I just realized," she said. "We're going to the rehearsal tomorrow, right? That means I'll get to see him."

"Maybe you can be his page turner," Nancy teased. "Anyway, what happened with you and Sasha?"

Bess shrugged and snitched a cookie from Nancy's plate. "Nothing happened. We were talking, and then Marina came up and the two of them had a kind of argument. Sasha forgot all about me. I got a little bored so I wandered around and met Yves."

"What were they arguing about?" Nancy bit into a slice of pineapple.

"Well, the conversation was mostly in Russian," Bess said, "but I think it was about how late they should stay tonight. I got the feeling that Marina's all work and no play and Sasha definitely likes to play."

"I think you're right," Nancy said, remembering what Sasha had told her earlier. Well, he could play all he wanted. But not with her.

* * *

Late the next morning Nancy and her friends drove to the dance institute to watch the dancers rehearse for a while. They'd made plans to take Sasha and Marina to the beach later in the day, so all three were wearing shorts and bright, loose-fitting T-shirts over their swimsuits.

"I wonder if Dmitri's going to come to the beach with us," Bess said. "He doesn't seem like the fun-in-the-sun type."

"I know what you mean." Nancy laughed. "He's sort of stiff and proper, like a military man. Sasha told me he used to be a pilot."

"Really?" George said. "No wonder he looks grumpy. He probably feels grounded."

"Sasha says he takes his job very seriously," Nancy said. "So I'm sure he'll come to the beach to keep an eye on things."

Bess grinned mischievously. "Maybe it'll loosen him up a little."

Nancy had her doubts about that, but she was glad the chaperon would be there, anyway. Maybe Sasha wouldn't flirt with her if Dmitri was around. If he did continue, she knew she'd have to tell him to stop. She was hoping the whole thing would just kind of fade away, though, especially when Sasha saw an entire beach full of great-looking girls.

"I can't wait to see Yves again," Bess said as they pulled up to the institute. "Do I look okay?"

"Great, as usual," George told her. "But we're here to watch the dancers, not the pianist, remember?"

"I think I can keep an eye on both." Bess squared her shoulders determinedly. "Come on, let's go."

When a new school had been built a few years earlier, the Cultural Society took over the old one. The society had renovated it to house a stage, a good-size auditorium, dressing rooms, rehearsal rooms, and a handsome lobby.

Once inside the girls heard the strains of piano music. Following the sound to the auditorium, they passed a room where several dancers were working at the barre, and another where they were working on new steps. Inside the auditorium Sasha and Marina were on the stage, loosening up for a pas de deux, which they were about to rehearse. In the front row, wearing a dark suit, was Dmitri Kolchak.

Dana Harding, who had planned the gala opening ballet and choreographed a couple of new dances, was standing just below the stage, a clipboard in her hands. After a brief conversation with Yves, she called out, "All right, dancers! Let's try it."

Sasha and Marina took their positions as Nancy, George, and Bess quietly sat down in a middle row. Yves struck a chord, and the two Soviet dancers went into action.

"Oh," Bess said after a minute, "they're fantastic!"

Nancy nodded, her eyes never leaving the stage. Even though Sasha and Marina were just learning the piece, and there were lots of stops and starts and conferences with Dana, Nancy could see why they were lead dancers.

Marina's all work and no play sure paid off. Dressed in black tights and leotard, the young ballerina was incredibly graceful as she moved across the stage in a series of pirouettes and quick, gliding steps.

As for Sasha, Nancy was almost over-whelmed by his abilities. He wasn't a cute flirt anymore—here he was all business. Wearing tights and a scruffy gray sweatshirt, Sasha leaped and whirled with such grace and power that Nancy realized she was holding her breath half the time.

As the music drew to its tempestuous con-clusion, Sasha sprang into a jeté, soaring through the air like a leaf on the wind. Nancy caught her breath, half expecting him to fly. After what seemed minutes, Sasha landed, and together he and Marina spun through the final steps of the pas de deux.

"Wonderful!" Dana called out after a mo-ment of appreciative silence. "Let's take a break, and then we'll meet in rehearsal room two to work out a few of those sticky places."

Marina nodded and left, her face cool and

aloof once again. Sasha leaped nimbly from the stage and reached for a towel that had been thrown over the back of a front row seat. Catching sight of Nancy, he grinned and winked at her.

Nancy couldn't help laughing. The old Sasha was back. But she had to admit to herself that the glimpse she had gotten of the new Sasha, the talented young artist, had been very stirring.

Draping the towel around his neck, Sasha started up the aisle toward her. Nancy was still smiling at him when she heard the auditorium door slam open with a loud bang.

Turning, she saw Gary standing there. His lean face was pale, and his eyes were wide with shock. He and Sasha reached the three girls at the same time.

"Gary, what's wrong?" George asked, standing up. "What's happened?"

"It's unbelievable!" Gary shook his head, gasping as if he'd just run a race. "It doesn't make any sense!"

"What doesn't?" George asked. "Come on, Gary, what is it?"

"I'm out," Gary said. "Suspended from Jetstream."

Bess gasped.

"Why, Gary?" Nancy asked.

Still shaking his head, Gary sank down in the aisle seat. "It's unbelievable," he said again. Looking over at Nancy, he tried to smile. "I'm glad you're a detective, because I think I'm going to need one."

"Will you please tell us what's going on?" George cried.

"Jetstream suspended me because they think I—" Gary took a deep breath. "Because they think I'm a spy."

Chapter

Four

THERE WERE a few seconds of complete silence while everyone stared at Gary. Finally George said, "You're right. That's totally unbelievable."

Bess nodded indignantly. "And ridiculous!"

"Yeah, but it's true," Gary said, his voice shaky. "Jetstream really believes I'm involved in some kind of industrial espionage."

"Why?" Nancy asked, scooting down the row to sit next to him. "They've got to have a reason, even if it sounds crazy."

"Sure they do," Gary told her. "And it *is* crazy." He took another deep breath and let it out in a big sigh. "Okay," he said. "Here goes.

Jetstream's biggest competition is this company in France called Aviane. Jetstream got wind that Aviane's almost ready to put a new plane on the market. And guess what it's like?"

"The secret one Jetstream's been working on?" George asked. "The Jetstar?"

"You got it," Gary said. "Jetstream figured there was no way for Aviane to have copied the Jetstar unless somebody on the inside fed them the plans."

"And they think it's you," Nancy said.

Gary nodded.

"But why?" Bess asked. "I mean, you're not the designer of the plane."

"No, but I could have gotten hold of the plans. Not that I did," he said. "Anyway, Jetstream found out about Aviane's new plane late yesterday. So they searched the entire plant for any clue as to who the spy was. I have a locker there—all the test pilots do. Are you ready for the crazy part?"

"They found something in your locker," Nancy said.

Gary nodded again. "A blueprint for the Jetstar."

"A plant!" Sasha said excitedly. "Whoever is really passing the plans to the French planted that blueprint in your locker. That must be it. Right, Nancy?"

Nancy had forgotten that Sasha was there. When she looked up at him, she saw that his blue eyes were bright with curiosity. Dmitri

33

and Yves had come up the aisle, too, and were standing close by, listening intently to every word.

"It had to be a plant," Gary said before Nancy had a chance to answer Sasha. *"I* sure didn't put it there." He shook his head sadly. "Anyway, when I went in this morning for my meeting, I got the third degree. Then I got suspended. I'm out. I can't even go back to the complex."

George took Gary's hand. *"You* might not be able to get in, but *we* can," she said. She looked at Nancy. "I think we should pay a visit to Jetstream, don't you?"

"Absolutely," Nancy agreed. "I don't know if they'll tell us anything, but it won't hurt to ask."

Gary managed a smile. "I was hoping you'd say that."

"You'd better go for a long swim, or a walk, or do something to calm yourself down," George told her boyfriend softly. "You look awfully tense."

Gary gave a short laugh. "Is that so surprising?" he asked.

"George and I will tell you the second we find out anything," Nancy said, trying to reassure him.

Taking Gary's arm, George led him to the door of the auditorium and kissed him briefly. "Don't worry," she said. "It must be a mistake."

After Gary left, Bess walked Nancy and George out to the car. "I'll stay and go with Sasha and Marina to the beach if you guys aren't back in time," she offered.

"Great," Nancy said. She climbed into the driver's seat and pulled away.

"Sasha was right," George said, as she and Nancy drove toward the Jetstream complex.

"Sasha was right about what?" Nancy asked.

"Somebody planted that blueprint in Gary's locker to make him look guilty," George said. "Gary flies planes, he doesn't design them. What would he be doing with a blueprint?"

"As he said, he could have gotten hold of it any time," Nancy reminded her. "And whoever's leaking the plans is probably getting a pile of money from Aviane. Test pilots don't make big salaries, do they?"

"Nancy!" George's dark eyes widened in shock. "You don't think he's guilty, do you? I know he isn't. He wouldn't do anything like this!"

"I'm just trying to think like Jetstream," Nancy explained.

Of course, she thought, she and George had known Gary for only a couple of weeks. They didn't know much about him, really, except that he'd grown up in Ohio and that he was friendly and easygoing. Friendly, easygoing people *did* commit crimes.

Still, he was so shocked and upset when he came to the institute that Nancy was almost positive he wasn't faking his innocence. She'd have to keep her eyes open, but she really believed he was innocent, and she hoped for George's sake she was right.

The Jetstream complex was about twenty minutes from the dance institute and was located in the middle of what had once been potato fields. It had its own airstrip and hangars, and the offices were in a low, sleek, tinted-glass building surrounded by a high metal fence.

Driving up to the main gate, Nancy realized they would probably need some kind of pass to get in. Sure enough, the guard immediately asked for them.

"We don't have any," Nancy told him. "But we're here to see Eileen Martin. She's expecting us." She told him their names and waited while the guard made a call from his phone. When he hung up, he wrote out two passes, gave them to Nancy, and waved them through the gate.

"I didn't know you'd called her," George said as Nancy drove into the parking lot.

"I didn't," Nancy said. "I just took a chance and kept my fingers crossed."

"Good idea," George remarked. "I know you'll find out who did this, and I also know it won't be Gary."

"Then let's get started," Nancy said.

Passing a large bronze sculpture of an airplane, the girls walked to the main entrance of the Jetstream building. Eileen Martin was waiting for them inside the glass doors.

"Well," she said with a laugh, "you're right on time!"

Nancy laughed, too. "Thanks for getting us in, Eileen."

"No problem," Eileen assured them as they started down a hallway. "I must say I was a little surprised, though. It's such a warm day, I thought you'd be at the beach."

"We're going later," Nancy said, glancing down at her white shorts and orange T-shirt. "We would have changed before we came, but we were kind of in a hurry."

"It's an emergency," George added.

"Sounds serious." Eileen led them into her office, which had a desk, a drafting table, file cabinets, and windows with a view of the bronze airplane sculpture. "What's it about?"

"Gary Powell," George said.

At the mention of Gary's name, Eileen's friendly expression changed. She frowned and pursed her lips, and her soft brown eyes seemed to get darker. "What a shame," she murmured. "Such a nice young man."

"He didn't do it," George told her. "He wouldn't."

"Oh, I hope you're right," Eileen said. "But I'm afraid Jetstream's convinced that he did. And the evidence is pretty damaging for him. I wonder how he's going to clear his name."

"That's why we're here," George said.

"Nancy especially. She's a detective, and she told Gary she'd try to find out what happened."

Eileen looked startled, then gave a little laugh. "That's right. Eloise mentioned your work, Nancy. I'd forgotten."

"George and I were hoping you might be able to help us," Nancy said. "Gary said you were a senior engineer here. Did you work on the plane?"

Eileen rolled her eyes. "I haven't worked on anything else for over two years," she said. "I'm still working on it."

"Then maybe you could tell us about it," Nancy suggested. "And about the blueprint they found in Gary's locker."

"Well, everyone here is under strict orders not to discuss it," Eileen said. "The president, Mr. Elkins, has been very specific about that."

"Maybe we should talk to him," Nancy suggested.

Eileen shook her head. "He's at a meeting in Washington, and he'll be away for four days." She sighed. "I *can* tell you that Jetstream is convinced they've found the leak—Gary. And now that they've got it plugged up, so to speak, we're going ahead to try to get our plane on the market before the competition does."

"Isn't Jetstream worried that if Gary's not the leak, then whoever is will get any new plans to Aviane?" Nancy asked.

Eileen frowned again and looked worried for a moment. Then she shook her head. "Jetstream must really be convinced that Gary's the one."

George started to protest but was interrupted when the phone buzzed. Eileen answered it, listened for a few seconds, then said, "All right, Bill, hold your horses. I'll bring it now."

She hung up and gathered some papers from her desk. "That was Bill Fairgate—he designed the Jetstar," she said. "Very impatient man. When he wants something, he wants it five minutes ago."

"I guess we'd better not keep you, then," Nancy said.

"Oh, dear, I'm afraid I haven't been any help at all." Eileen sighed. "It's just such a sticky situation—I'm sure you understand." Clipping the papers together, she went to the door. "Bill's office is on the way, so why don't you come with me? I'll drop these off and then show you out."

Leaving Eileen's office, the three of them walked back down the hall. George looked disappointed, but Nancy was glad for the chance to meet the Jetstar's designer. Maybe she could get something out of him.

Bill Fairgate was in his forties, Nancy guessed, short and stocky and extremely grumpy looking. He barely nodded when

Eileen introduced them, but when she told him that Nancy was a detective, he actually laughed.

"Jetstream hired you a little late, didn't they?" he asked sarcastically. "The horse is already out of the barn."

"I'm investigating on my own," Nancy told him. "I don't work for Jetstream."

"Smart girl," Bill muttered. "Anyone who does work for this company ought to have his head examined."

What's eating him? Nancy wondered.

"Now, Bill!" Eileen laughed, but Nancy could tell she was embarrassed.

"Come on, Eileen," he said. "You know what I'm talking about. This place was asking for it—"

"Bill!" Eileen interrupted again, handing him the papers. "Excuse us just a moment," she said to the girls.

She and Bill bent their heads together and conferred quietly. George and Nancy waited by his desk, which was near the door. The desk was a mess, with papers and used coffee cups cluttering the entire top.

Without really meaning to, Nancy found herself reading a memo that was sticking out from a sloppy heap of papers. The memo was addressed to Bill Fairgate and was dated four months earlier.

"Dear Bill," it went. "Regarding your last memo, I'm afraid Jetstream must turn down your request for a raise at this time. As I've told you, this in no way means that we don't appreciate your valuable contribution in designing the Jetstar."

So Bill Fairgate had asked for more money and been turned down, Nancy thought, sneaking a glance at him. That might explain why he was such a grump.

There was more on the memo, but it was hidden. Nancy took hold of a corner of it. She was just about to give it a gentle tug when she became aware of the silence in the office.

Glancing up, Nancy saw that Eileen was still looking at the papers she'd brought in. But Bill Fairgate was looking at Nancy. His eyes were narrowed to slits, and his expression was no longer grumpy. It was furious. Furious *and* frightened, Nancy thought.

Nancy wondered if Bill Fairgate was more than just a grouch. Could he have been so fed up with Jetstream that he'd decided to sell his talents to another company? A French company named Aviane?

Chapter

Five

GIVING BILL FAIRGATE her most innocent smile, Nancy shuffled the pile of papers into shape. "Sorry," she said apologetically. "I'm an awful klutz. I nearly knocked these off your desk just now."

Bill still glowered at her, but slowly the suspicious gleam left his eye. He grunted and turned back to Eileen.

George was gazing questioningly at Nancy. "We should go," Nancy told her briskly. "Eileen and Mr. Fairgate must have tons of things to do. Thanks for your help, Eileen."

"I only wish there was more I could do for

poor Gary," Eileen told the girls. "Please let me know if you come up with any other leads."

"Well, that didn't get us anywhere," George complained as she and Nancy drove back to the dance institute. "I was really hoping Eileen could help us. I thought she would, since she likes Gary so much. I guess she's just scared of getting into trouble with Jetstream. So we're still at square one." She frowned.

"Maybe not," Nancy said. She told George about the memo and Bill Fairgate's reaction to her reading it. "He definitely has a big gripe with Jetstream, and it's about money."

"Aviane must be paying a bundle for those plans!" George said excitedly. "That gives Bill Fairgate a really strong motive. This is great!"

"Don't start celebrating yet," Nancy said. "It's just a possibility."

"Don't worry," George told her. "I know we don't have any proof, but Gary and the two pilots he rooms with are really good friends. I know they'll want to help him. Maybe they can find out about Bill Fairgate for us—like whether he just bought a new car or house or something really expensive."

"Good thinking," Nancy agreed.

"Why don't you drop me off at Gary's so I can tell him?" George suggested. "I know I'm supposed to go to the beach with you guys, but . . ."

"Don't worry about it," Nancy said. "Finding whoever sold those plans is more important. Be careful, though," she warned. "As far as Jetstream is concerned, Gary's the guilty one. If he gets caught snooping around, he'll be in more trouble than he already is."

After dropping George off at the small house Gary shared with two other pilots, Nancy hurried back to the dance institute.

Opening the door, she saw Dmitri, Marina, and a French dancer—Jacques somebody, whom she'd met the previous night—standing just outside the auditorium. As she walked toward them, she could hear that they were speaking in French. They spoke much too quickly for her to follow, but it was obvious that the conversation was serious—all three were wearing frowns, and their voices were low and intense.

All at once the three of them caught sight of Nancy and stopped talking immediately. Dmitri nodded to her, and Marina and Jacques stared at the floor.

"Hi," Nancy said. "Am I interrupting something?"

"Not at all." Dmitri gave her a small smile. "We were discussing—"

"Sasha," Marina finished with a sniff. "The rehearsal is over, and he is looking for you."

"Oh." They must be convinced I'm interested in Sasha, Nancy thought. I caught them gossiping about it with Jacques, and now they're embarrassed. She wanted to set them straight, but first she had to set Sasha straight.

"Well," she said cheerfully, "I'm here. And pretty soon we'll *all* go to the beach."

Smiling brightly, she pushed open the auditorium door and stepped inside. Several dancers were still on the stage, chatting together. Bess was down in the front row, as close to the piano as she could get, Nancy noticed. Yves wasn't there at the moment, but Nancy decided he must be coming back. Otherwise Bess wouldn't be sitting so patiently.

"Hi," she said when she reached Bess. "I guess I made it back in time for the beach."

"Nancy, hi!" Bess stood up, her face anxious. "What happened? Where's George? Did you find anything out?"

"George is with Gary," Nancy said. "And I'm not sure if we learned anything or not. I'll tell you everything later, okay? Let's get to the beach. Where's Sasha?"

"He just went in to change," Bess said as the two of them headed up the aisle. "He's been asking for you about every fifteen minutes."

"So I've heard." Nancy lifted her eyebrows.

They were halfway up the aisle when suddenly a voice burst out angrily in French, *"Attention, s'il vous plaît!"*

Turning around, they saw Yves standing by his piano, holding pages of sheet music in his hands. "My music, it has been disarranged

45

completely!" he said, switching to English. "I must insist it be left alone. The stage is your territory," he went on, gesturing to the dancers. "The piano is mine. Please, do not disturb my music." He stopped and took a deep breath. *"Merci,"* he added.

Bess's cheeks turned pink. "That was me," she whispered to Nancy. "I knocked his music off the rack when I was looking through it during the break. Do you think I should confess?"

"I'd say don't tell him, if you want him to go on liking you. Talk about touchy!" Nancy whispered back.

"I know. I thought the dancers would be the temperamental ones," Bess agreed. They pushed through the swinging doors that led to the dressing rooms. "But Yves is an artist, too. He says accompanists are completely misunderstood."

Nancy suppressed a grin. She suspected Yves was a bit of a blowhard. She hoped Bess's crush would fade painlessly as she got to know him better.

"Does that mean you managed to talk to him during rehearsal?" she asked.

"Every chance I got," Bess said with a smile.

"This is fantastic!" Sasha stretched his arms out toward the ocean. Beads of water dripped from his hair, and sand was clinging to his muscular legs. "I could stay here forever!"

46

Nancy laughed. "That's exactly what Bess said. I don't know if we'll ever get her back to River Heights."

"I must go in again!" Sasha said exuberantly. Grabbing Nancy's hand, he pulled her with him, and the two of them dashed across the sand and into the cool surf.

Diving underwater they came up laughing and waited for a good wave. Catching one finally, they body-surfed back to shore. Scrambling to her feet, Nancy pushed her hair out of her face and waited for Sasha to get up.

"Enough," she said. "I didn't have any lunch and I'm starving. Let's get something to eat."

Nancy *was* hungry, but she had another reason for wanting to go to the concession stand. Somehow, she and Sasha had wound up alone together, and she didn't want it to stay that way.

They hadn't come together. The institute had provided Dmitri with a car, and much to Nancy's amusement, he'd insisted on driving Marina and Sasha to the beach instead of letting them go with Nancy and Bess. So Nancy had taken three other dancers—two Canadians and a beautiful Japanese girl—instead.

It was time to join a crowd, she decided. "Come on," she said. "I'll buy you a hot dog."

"All right," Sasha said, shaking the water from his arms. "And I must ask you about your case. I would have before, but the ocean distracted me. Tell me everything you learned this morning."

"Well, I learned that Jetstream is convinced Gary leaked the plans," Nancy told him, as they threaded their way between sunbathers stretched out on colorful beach towels.

"But you?" Sasha asked, picking up his towel and drying himself. "Are you convinced?"

Nancy dried off, too. "I have a lot of doubts," she said, tossing her towel down and taking her coin purse out of her beach bag. "Jetstream should, too. After all, they're still working on the plane. If Gary's not the leak, and Aviane gets hold of any plans after this, Jetstream's really going to look pretty foolish."

Sasha nodded. "The trick is to learn exactly what has been leaked and what might be leaked in the future," he said as they walked on. "I would start with the plans themselves."

"So would I," Nancy agreed. "If I could get my hands on them."

"You see?" he asked with a grin. "We think alike. I told you I love mysteries. You should let me help you."

"Thanks, but you've got your hands full with the rehearsals," she said. "I saw you dance this morning, Sasha, and I don't think Dmitri needs to worry about you disgracing your country. You're wonderful."

"Thank you. A compliment from you means

a lot." They were climbing over a dune, and Sasha reached out for Nancy's hand. "Nancy," he said. "You must let me tell you something. I have met a lot of girls on my travels, and I admit, I have flirted a lot."

Nancy swallowed. His blue eyes were so serious. She knew she should stop him now, before he said anything he might regret, but something held her back for a moment. Maybe I just want to hear him flatter me, she thought guiltily. Maybe I just like the attention!

"I admit, too, that I have flirted with you," Sasha went on. "But it was not in fun, like the others. Nancy, I am—"

"Sasha, wait." Nancy freed her hand and took a deep breath. It was time to set him straight. "I like you a lot," she said, "but I have a boyfriend. Back in River Heights. His name is Ned, and we've been together for a long time."

"Are you getting bored with him, maybe?" Sasha asked hopefully.

Nancy shook her head, almost wishing she had a different answer for him. "No, I'm not. I like you and I want to have fun, Sasha, but I think you should find someone else to flirt with."

"So." Sasha stood still, thinking a minute. Then he nodded, his light brown hair shining in the sun. "I think you want me to back off. Okay. I will." He reached out and draped his towel around Nancy's neck, pulling her a little closer to him. "For now I will back off," he said. "But not forever."

With another grin, he turned and sprinted up the beach toward the concession stand. Nancy followed more slowly, his towel still around her neck. The conversation hadn't gone exactly the way she'd planned. She had the feeling Sasha wasn't convinced about her feelings for Ned. Well, that's his problem, she thought. At least she'd told him.

The concession stand was busy, and Nancy found most of the others from the institute there. Everybody seemed to have gotten hungry at the same time. Bess was there, drinking a diet soda and talking with the two Canadian dancers they had driven to the beach. Both guys, of course.

Sasha had just joined Marina and Dmitri, who were standing with Jacques, the dancer from France. Dmitri hadn't been swimming, but he *was* wearing shorts and a T-shirt. Maybe he's unbending a little, Nancy thought with a smile.

Tying Sasha's towel around her waist, Nancy got in line and bought a soda and three hot dogs. Two were for her, and the third was for Sasha. When she turned around, she didn't see him. The two men were gone, too, but she did catch a glimpse of Marina, dressed in a rose-colored swimsuit, heading for the parking area. They must be leaving. It was funny that Sasha hadn't told her.

Hungrily, Nancy wolfed down one hot dog in about five bites. Balancing the other two and the can of soda, she started after Marina.

When she got to the parking area, she saw Marina and Sasha standing beside a bank of pay phones. Their gestures told her they were having a heated discussion of some kind. Sasha glanced up, spotted Nancy, and beckoned her over.

"Are you going?" Nancy called. She stepped onto the hot asphalt. As she winced at the sudden pain in her bare feet, she heard a scream.

Marina was screaming and staring directly at Nancy, an expression of horror on her beautiful face.

Then Nancy heard the car. It was off to her left, moving straight at her, coming fast. She could tell from the sound that it wouldn't stop.

Chapter

Six

DROPPING THE SODA, Nancy dove for the sand, the hot dogs flying out of her hands and arcing away. The sharp grains bit into her bare legs and arms as she skidded over the sand. Tumbling, she heard another scream and thought it must be Marina again. Then, finally, she heard the car brake. It screeched hideously, showering her with more sand before it finally came to a stop.

Breathing hard, Nancy slowly got to her feet. The car was exactly where she'd been standing seconds before, the soda can flattened under its right front wheel.

The car doors flew open, and Dmitri and Jacques scrambled out. They were shouting in a mixture of English, Russian, and French.

"Nancy!" Sasha called, hurrying over to her. "Are you okay?"

"Scratched up a bit," she said. "But okay. What happened?"

Dmitri, Jacques, and Marina joined them, and the chaperon spoke quickly in Russian, gesturing toward the car a lot.

"He's too upset to think properly in English," Marina told Nancy. "He says that the car just took off."

"I felt it, too," Jacques said. "It simply surged forward."

"I've heard of that happening," Nancy said, brushing sand off her arms. "I think you'd better leave the car here. I can take you wherever you were going."

"Dmitri was giving me a ride back to the institute," Jacques put in quickly. "I have an extra rehearsal this afternoon."

Nancy shrugged. "I'll give you a ride. Mr. Kolchak, if you call the rental company, they'll come for this car and give you another one."

"Yes," Dmitri said. "I will do exactly that. I must apologize, Miss Drew. Are you sure you're not hurt?"

"Yes, and please don't apologize," Nancy said. "It wasn't your fault."

Looking at Dmitri and Jacques, Nancy did

wonder—had it really been an accident? She thought cars that went out of control had all been recalled. Was there another faulty batch of them on the road, or had the "accident" been deliberate?

"Just an accident, definitely," Bess said. "Really, Nancy, I can't believe Jacques is involved in espionage."

Nancy and Bess had taken Jacques to the institute before dropping Dmitri, Sasha, and Marina off at their house. Now they were on their way back to Eloise's.

"He does seem to spend a lot of time with Marina and Dmitri, even though—as far as I know—they never met before this program started," Nancy reasoned out loud. "And I told you how they stopped talking the second they saw me at the rehearsal."

"So? Maybe they were just gossiping and didn't want you to hear."

"Dmitri used to be a pilot, Bess. He knows planes. And Sasha said they were going to France next. Who knows? Maybe Dmitri will be taking some Jetstream plans with him. And why was Dmitri giving Jacques a ride back, anyway? It's very unlike him to leave Sasha and Marina alone for even a few minutes."

"Hold it," Bess interrupted. "There could be other explanations, you know. Maybe Marina and Jacques are interested in each other—

maybe that's why he hangs around the Soviets so much. They're not the only ones going to France next— all the dancers are. Jacques did have a rehearsal this afternoon—I heard Dana telling him to be back early. Maybe Dmitri was just being nice."

"I know, I know," Nancy agreed.

"Besides," Bess went on, "the car accident happened after you told Sasha about your visit to Jetstream. What are you saying? That Sasha told Dmitri and then Dmitri and Jacques decided to scare you?"

Nancy shook her head. She wasn't sure. Her idea that Dmitri and Jacques were go-betweens for Bill Fairgate (or someone at Jetstream) and Aviane *did* seem kind of far-fetched. But the theory was possible, and as long as it *was* possible, she decided she'd better be careful. More than a soda can might get crushed the next time.

When Nancy and Bess got home, they found Eileen Martin sitting with Eloise in the white, sunny kitchen. The two women were drinking iced tea and going over a sample program of the institute's opening performance.

"Nancy, Bess!" Eloise stood up, a look of concern on her face. "Eileen told me about Gary. I simply can't believe it. George must be so upset."

"She is," Nancy agreed. "Is she back yet?"

"No, but she called just a little bit ago,"

Eloise said. "She told me to tell you that she and Gary uncovered something."

"Does that mean they're trying to investigate this themselves?" Eileen asked.

"Well, Gary's reputation is on the line," Nancy said, wondering what he and George had found out about Bill Fairgate. "And he's out of a job. He must feel he has to do something."

Eileen nodded, frowning. "I can understand that," she said. "But I'm not so sure it's a wise idea. He might get himself into more trouble."

"How could he get into more trouble than he's already in?" Bess asked, taking two glasses from the cupboard and pouring Nancy and herself some tea.

"Because if he's not the leak," Nancy explained, "then whoever is might do just about anything to stop Gary from finding that out."

Bess looked worried, but Eileen laughed. "Heavens, I didn't mean it that way!" she said. "I just meant that Gary should probably have a detective do his investigating for him, that's all."

"He does," Bess said. "He's got Nancy. If anyone can get to the bottom of this, she can."

"I'm sure she can. It's just that Jetstream thinks it's already gotten to the bottom of the question." Eileen smiled at Nancy. "You must think they're wrong."

"I'm not sure of anything yet," Nancy said,

taking a sip of tea. "But I'm going to keep on digging until I am sure."

Eileen left a few minutes later, and soon after that, George and Gary arrived in Gary's car.

"Guess what?" George said excitedly as the two of them burst into the kitchen. "Bill Fairgate's really into the stock market."

"One of my buddies, another pilot," Gary said, "told me that Fairgate's always giving him tips, telling him what stocks are up or down and what to invest in." He slapped the table in satisfaction. "It's got to be him!"

Nancy tried to smile, but she knew Gary's information wasn't really incriminating. So Bill Fairgate liked to play the stock market. It might show that he was eager to make lots of money, but it certainly wasn't illegal. Gary was just eager to place the blame on the first likely person to come along. Not that Nancy could blame him.

"What is it, Nan?" George asked, frowning. "Don't tell me you don't think this is important."

Nancy sighed. Things would be a lot easier if Gary wasn't George's boyfriend. George was on his side, of course, but Nancy had to try to keep an open mind.

"It could be important," Nancy said. "But we need a lot more before we can accuse Bill Fairgate of anything. It would be nice if he'd just invested a huge amount of money," she added with a smile.

"We can try to find that out," Gary said.

"Okay," Nancy agreed. "But I keep thinking we're starting in the middle instead of the beginning. I wish there was some way to see the Jetstar plans. If we could figure out what was leaked, we might be able to figure out who leaked it."

"Maybe this will help," Eloise said. She'd been listening quietly, clearing off the table, and now she held up that day's newspaper. "'Jetstream Fends Off Challenge in Race for Skies,'" she read.

Everyone crowded around Eloise as she read the article aloud. "'Aviane, France's leading designer-manufacturer of jet planes, said in a surprise announcement today that it is nearing completion of a plane it hopes will corner the highly lucrative market of small, privately owned business jets.

"'Aviane didn't reveal the plans for its plane, but it did say that the new jet contains innovations that are sure to have similar businesses scrambling to catch up.

"'It is well-known that Jetstream, a local company and a fierce competitor of Aviane's, has been developing a similar plane for almost three years. Asked about the possibility of industrial espionage, a spokesman for Jetstream refused to comment, saying only that its plane, the Jetstar, would be ready for the market in the very near future. The spokesman also said that Jetstream had full confidence in its ability to head off Aviane's challenge.'"

Eloise shook her head. "I guess it doesn't really tell us much."

"Except that Jetstream's closed the book on me," Gary commented bitterly.

"This reporter," Nancy said, looking at the paper. "Susan Wexler. She sounds like she suspects something. I wonder if I could talk to her."

"Well, she lives right here in the Hamptons," Eloise told her. "I met her once. She's a very nice young woman. Let me get her number for you."

"Thanks, Aunt Eloise. Maybe I can meet with her tonight." Nancy thought a minute. "We're taking Sasha and Marina to the Lobster Tank tonight. Maybe Susan Wexler can meet us there."

"I don't think Gary and I are in the mood for a place with loud rock music," George said.

"Oh, you have to come!" Bess said.

"Maybe you should," Nancy agreed. "It hasn't exactly been a great day for you. Maybe some music will help you forget for a while."

"Right," Bess said. "It'll be fun, you'll see. A lot of people from the institute will be there."

George laughed wryly. "Yves Goulard, too?"

"Well, naturally," Bess said with a conspiratorial grin. "That's *why* it's going to be so much fun."

Nancy drove George, Gary, and Bess to the Lobster Tank in her little rented Honda, stopping off at the house where the Soviet dancers were staying. The plan had been for Bess to borrow Dmitri's car to drive Sasha and Marina to the club, but Dmitri wouldn't allow that.

"I will take Sasha and Marina," he declared, drawing his beetling brows together. "They should not go out unsupervised."

"Wow, you'd think Dmitri was a KGB agent or something, the way he watches those two," Bess commented.

Nancy nodded, glancing in the rearview mirror to make sure Dmitri was still behind her. He had gotten a new rental car, a dark blue sedan. He was still there. Nancy turned her gaze away almost instantly. Dmitri's high beams practically blinded her. "Maybe he is KGB. Maybe he's afraid they'll defect," she suggested, smiling.

The Lobster Tank wasn't fancy; it was in a plain, weather-beaten building and served only pretzels and soda. It did have live music, though, and plenty of room to dance, and it was one of the most popular clubs in the Hamptons. The band that night was called Blackjack, and by the time Nancy arrived, the place was jumping.

"Oh, look, everybody from the institute's here," Bess said excitedly. She pointed out a pretty, petite girl with dark blond hair who was dancing with a handsome guy with a sullen face. "There's Emily Terner, and her boyfriend, Keith—cute, but kind of a jerk. And there's Jacques. . . . And there's Yves!" Bess waved to the handsome, dark-eyed accompanist. Smoothing back her blond hair, she started across the dance floor toward him, moving in time to the music.

Gary took George's hand. "Come on," he said, "let's dance. Maybe Nancy and Bess are right, that it'll take our minds off this rotten day."

Sasha, looking great in jeans and a black T-shirt, turned to Nancy, smiling. "This is a wonderful place!" he shouted over the music. "I'm going to dance until I drop!"

Even Marina looked excited at the scene. She stood tapping her foot to the pulsing beat of the music, and when Sasha grabbed her hand and pulled her onto the floor, she threw back her head and laughed with pleasure.

Nancy hid her surprise that Sasha hadn't asked *her* to dance. Oh, well, why should she mind? Anyway, she had other things to think about.

Dmitri sat down by himself at an empty table and glowered as his charges enjoyed themselves on the dance floor. Nancy's interest was caught for a second by Jacques as he approached Dmitri's table, but the French dancer merely smiled and walked on by.

Nancy bought a soda and checked her watch. She'd reached the reporter, Susan Wexler, who'd been eager to talk about Jetstream—especially after Nancy had told her that a Jetstream pilot would be part of the group. She wouldn't be there for another half hour, so Nancy found a table and sat down to watch the action.

The place was packed. After twenty minutes, Nancy lost track of almost everyone except Sasha. He was easy to spot, moving through the crowd, dancing with just about everyone. He danced as well to rock as to ballet music, and Nancy had trouble keeping her eyes off him. At least, she thought, he's been keeping his promise about backing off.

Sasha whirled in time to the music and caught Nancy staring at him. He grinned and waved—and then he winked.

Nancy shook her head, smiling to herself. Sasha might be backing off, but he wasn't giving up. Nancy had the feeling he'd be at her side before long, so she decided to take a quick walk outside. She could use some fresh air.

The Lobster Tank was right at the edge of an inlet, and the breeze felt sticky with salt but cool. Nancy was thinking about Jetstream, when she noticed a piece of paper stuck under the windshield wiper of her car.

Probably from the Lobster Tank, she

thought, advertising a new band or something. She pulled the paper off and looked at it.

Scrawled across the back of a flyer, in black Magic Marker, was her name. Underneath it was a warning: "Stop now your investigation of Jetstream or you will regret it. Curious detectives do not die of old age."

Chapter

Seven

WHAT IS THAT in your hand?"

Nancy jumped, whirled around, and came face-to-face with Sasha. Directly behind him were Marina and Dmitri.

"Sasha, you shouldn't sneak up on people like that!" Nancy said. "What are you doing out here, anyway?"

"I didn't mean to startle you," he told her. "I saw you come out and was afraid you were leaving before I had a chance to say good night. Dmitri was afraid to let me come by myself, I think, so he followed me."

"Sasha!" Dmitri growled. "You did not tell

me where you were going. It is my job to make
sure you do not come to harm."

Ignoring Dmitri's excuse, Sasha pointed to
the flyer in Nancy's hand. "What is that?" he
asked again.

Before Nancy could say anything, Sasha had
taken the paper from her and was reading it.
Then, with an air of triumph, he showed it to
Marina and Dmitri.

"You see?" he said to them. "Didn't I tell
you this was a true mystery?" He turned back
to Nancy, his eyes sparkling. "This is an
exciting development, isn't it?"

Nancy snatched the paper back. "I hardly
call having my life threatened an 'exciting
development,' Sasha."

"I must agree with Miss Drew," Dmitri said.

"I, too, Sasha." Marina's dark eyes were
flashing. Nancy wasn't sure if she was frightened or angry. "This is not a game."

"Such stays-in-the-mud," Sasha said, sighing dramatically.

"It's 'sticks-in-the-mud,'" Nancy said.
"And Marina's right. This isn't a game."

Dmitri nodded. "Sasha, Miss Drew is the
detective. You are the dancer. Come."

With a rueful smile, Sasha started to follow
them inside. Suddenly he bolted and ran back
to Nancy's side. Dmitri and Marina stopped to
wait for him, but Nancy saw that when Dmitri
tried to go after Sasha, Marina put a hand on
Dmitri's arm to stop him.

"I can see this in you, Nancy," Sasha said, touching her shoulder. "You are not one to give up. That note may frighten you, but it won't stop you."

Nancy nodded. "You're right. It won't stop me."

"Then you must be careful," he said. He squeezed her shoulder.

"Don't worry, Sasha." Nancy smiled. "I'm always careful."

She thought he'd leave then, but instead he said, "Let me help you, Nancy."

"What?"

"Please." Sasha's voice vibrated with excitement. "I know you must have many ideas about this case. So do I. That note—there's something extremely strange about it, don't you agree? I'm not sure what it is yet, but it might turn out to be a clue. Two heads are better than one, Nancy. Let us solve this case together."

He really means it, Nancy thought. She sighed. There was something so appealing, so vital about Sasha. It went beyond his incredible good looks—it had something to do with his character. If only . . .

No. Nancy sighed again. "Sasha, thanks, but I can't work that way."

"You always work alone?" he asked, his eyebrows lifting. "You never take help, even when it is offered?"

"No, that's not what I mean," Nancy protested. "But you read this note. I don't really think anybody's out to get me, but I'm not going to take any chances. And I'm sure not going to let you take any. Dmitri's right—I'm the detective and you're the dancer. Let's keep it that way, okay?"

Without waiting for a reply, Nancy walked directly back to the club. She reached the door at the same time as another young woman. The woman had light brown hair and a determined look in her green eyes. She stared at Nancy's hair and then pointed to her blouse. "White cotton with embroidered flowers, and red hair in a French braid. You must be Nancy Drew."

"And you must be Susan Wexler," Nancy said with a laugh.

"Right," Susan said, stepping aside to let the three Soviets go in. "Come on. Let's find a table and talk about Jetstream."

At the word *Jetstream,* both Dmitri and Sasha turned and stared at the two young women. For a second Nancy was afraid Sasha would try to join them. She breathed a sigh of relief when he grabbed Marina's hand and pulled her onto the dance floor again.

Spotting George and Gary, Nancy waved them over and soon the four of them were seated around a table, discussing Jetstream. Gary agreed to do an interview with Susan the next morning, on the condition that it wouldn't be published for a week. He was counting on Nancy's solving the case, and his story being scrapped for something bigger. Susan wasn't happy with this arrangement, but she agreed to it.

"I can't get a straight story out of *anyone*. None of the brass at Jetstar will talk to me, either," she complained. "They've always been secretive, but now it's ridiculous. I'm sure something's going on."

The band started a loud number, and Nancy almost had to shout. "Your article said Aviane wouldn't reveal its plans," she said. "But did they tell you anything 'off the record' that you can't print?"

Taking a sip of soda, Susan nodded. "Something about the engines. That's all they'd say. It's not much to go on. You know what I think? They were bluffing. I got the impression that it wasn't all going as smoothly as Aviane would like us to think. I don't believe they have all the bugs worked out of the system yet."

Nancy didn't respond, but she did feel a little glow of excitement. Susan and she were thinking along the same lines. That meant she might be on to something!

Engines, she mused. It could be in the design, which would be Bill Fairgate's territory. Or the engineering. Eileen Martin would know about that.

"Listen," Susan said, "you told me you're a detective. You're not asking these questions just because you're curious, right?"

"Right," Nancy admitted, glancing at Gary and George. "I think something fishy's going on, too. But I'm afraid I can't tell you any more."

"How about this?" asked Susan. "I'll keep bugging Jetstream to tell me what's going on. Maybe my editor will even let me do another story, just to keep them on their toes. I'll share anything I find out with you. If you learn anything, you tell me first."

"It's a deal," Nancy said with a grin.

Susan left a few minutes later, and Gary turned to Nancy. "I hope she never gets around to publishing my story," he said. "When Jetstream fired me, they said they'd keep the whole thing quiet as long as they got their plane out before Aviane did." He shook his head. "I'd really hate for my parents to read about this. I haven't told them yet."

"Maybe you won't have to," Nancy told him. She pulled the warning note out of her pocket and showed it to her friends. "I found this on my car a little while ago," she said. "I don't know who wrote it, but I'll find out. And when I do, you'll be cleared, Gary."

Gary looked relieved, but George frowned. "Whoever wrote this had to know you'd be here tonight," she said. "I guess that lets Bill Fairgate off the hook."

Nancy shook her head. "Not if he's working with somebody else. I don't think all the plans have been leaked yet. I'm not saying it's Bill

Fairgate, but whoever it is could be leaking them to a go-between."

"So what do we do now?" George asked.

"I need to know more about those Jetstar plans," Nancy said. "They're the key to what's being leaked." Suddenly she stood up. "You guys dance some more," she told them. "I'm going for a drive. This band is great, but I need quiet to think tonight. If I'm not back when you're ready to leave, make sure Bess gets a ride home."

Grabbing a handful of pretzels, Nancy left the Lobster Tank and got into her car. The Jetstream complex was probably locked up like a fort, and she knew she couldn't get in that night. Every fort had a weak spot, though, and Nancy was determined to find Jetstream's.

The jet manufacturing company was about a fifteen-minute drive from the Lobster Tank. Nancy cruised slowly by the front gate, which was lit by so many floodlights it looked as if it were noon instead of ten o'clock at night. Nancy didn't see a guard as she drove by, but she was sure one had to be around somewhere.

She kept on driving until she came to a place where she could safely pull off the road. Across from her was the fenced-in Jetstream complex. There were lights dotted along the fence, but they were spaced far enough apart so that there were long patches of darkness.

Wishing she wasn't wearing white, Nancy got out of the car and crossed the road to the fence. It was high, but it was chain link. Easy to climb, she thought. She was tempted, but she decided not to risk it. Not only did she have to get inside the grounds, she would have to get into the building, and even if she found a way, she wasn't going to do it right then.

Keeping an eye on the building, Nancy moved on down the fence. After a couple of minutes she spotted an entrance into the building. There was a single light above it, but the door itself was in shadow at the bottom of a couple of steps. Perfect, Nancy thought. There was probably an alarm, though. There were probably alarms all over the place.

She'd have to ask Gary. They tested planes at night, and he must have been there then. He might know something about the security system.

Satisfied that she'd at least found a door that wasn't lit up like a Christmas tree, Nancy started back to her car.

She was about halfway there when she heard it: a thumping, slapping sound behind her in the dirt. It was just a few feet away and coming closer.

Then Nancy heard the breathing, and by the time she figured out what it was, it was too late. A dog burst out of the darkness into a circle of light, stopping just two feet from her. Its lips were drawn back in a vicious snarl, and its dark, sleek body was quivering with tension. It was ready to spring!

71

Chapter

Eight

Nancy stopped moving. The dog, sensing no immediate danger, checked itself and didn't spring, but the deep rumbling in its chest got louder and louder until the dog burst out in a series of wild, angry barks. Each time it barked, the dog lifted its front feet off the ground, but it didn't go any closer.

Nancy remained perfectly still. She was almost afraid to breathe for fear the dog might decide it was a threatening action. The warning note flashed through her mind—"Curious detectives do not die of old age." Whoever had written it just might turn out to be right.

The wind picked up and whipped a loose

strand of hair across Nancy's eyes. Without thinking, she reached up to brush it away. The dog tensed again, and Nancy was sure it was going to attack when suddenly a man shouted, "Gina! Hold!"

The barking stopped immediately. A man wearing a guard's uniform walked up to the dog and patted it on the head. He kept his eyes on Nancy, and so did the dog.

"What are you doing here, miss?"

"I—"

"You couldn't be lost," he interrupted. "There's no place around here for you to be going to."

Nancy decided not to say anything to that.

"Come with me, please," he said. Snapping a leash on the dog's collar, he took Nancy's arm and the three of them started off.

"Look, I admit I was walking around the fence," Nancy said. "But I didn't go inside the fence and I haven't done anything wrong. I left my car off the road—back there. Why don't you just take me to it and I'll leave?"

"Can't let you do that yet," the guard said. "I have to check with the other guards to make sure security hasn't been breached. I left the walkie-talkie in my booth when I came to get Gina. It won't take long. *If* everything's okay," he added.

Nancy knew she hadn't breached security. She just hoped nobody else had, or she'd be in big trouble.

After a minute or two of walking, they came to another gate, near the complex's floodlit parking lot. The guard unlocked the gate and motioned Nancy inside. They walked past the parking lot to what looked like a tollbooth. The guard stepped inside the booth and got busy on his walkie-talkie.

Nancy watched the guard, and Gina watched Nancy. Don't get your hopes up, Nancy told the dog silently. You'll have to settle for a biscuit for dessert tonight.

After a few minutes the guard came out. "Looks like it's your lucky night," he said. "You're off the hook. I'll take you back to your car."

He took hold of the dog's leash again and they walked across the center of the complex toward the main gate. There were lights around the airplane sculpture Nancy and George had seen earlier. As they got up to it, Nancy saw words inscribed on its base. Slowing her steps, she was able to read them.

To the Memory of David Martin, Test Pilot, the inscription read. Died in Service to Jetstream. We Salute His Courage.

Below those words were the dates of David Martin's birth and death. He'd died two years before.

"Excuse me," Nancy said as they walked on. "That memorial to David Martin. Was he Eileen Martin's son?"

74

"That's right," the guard said. "He was testing a plane and something went wrong. It looked like he was going to bring it in safely, but the plane exploded when it touched down."

Nancy understood why Eileen was so motherly to all the test pilots. But what she couldn't understand was why Eileen wasn't fighting tooth and nail to clear Gary's name. Oh, she seemed sympathetic and concerned, but she wasn't doing anything about it. Maybe she believed he was guilty.

Back at Nancy's car, the guard turned to her. "Okay, here's the deal," he said. "You get in your car and you drive away from Jetstream."

Nancy nodded and got in. She wasn't about to argue. She'd been lucky and she knew it.

"And," the guard added in a warning tone, "you stay away. I won't forget you, and neither will Gina."

Nodding again, Nancy started the car. As she turned around and pulled away, she could see the guard and the dog in her rearview mirror, watching.

She wouldn't forget them, either, she thought. But she would be back.

Nancy drove slowly down the long road that fronted the Jetstream complex. It was late, but she didn't want to hurry. She wanted time to think.

The place was well guarded, but no place

was perfect. That door she'd spotted just before being caught was the one to use, *if* she could get to it.

She hadn't seen the guard turn off any alarms when they went through the gate, so maybe the fence wasn't wired. That meant she could just climb over. Of course the building itself probably did have alarms. She'd have to ask Gary about that.

When the guard had been on his walkie-talkie, Nancy had been able to hear him. He'd contacted two others. That made three guards all together.

As for Gina, she was a trained guard dog. She couldn't be bribed with a nice piece of steak. Were there more like her? It wouldn't be easy, but Nancy could deal with locked doors and even alarm systems. Dogs like Gina were another story.

She knew she'd think of something because she had to get her hands on the Jetstar plans. Jetstream wasn't ready to put the new plane on the market yet, so if Aviane was getting plans from Jetstream they wouldn't have the most up-to-date ones. The Jetstar was already built; it had even been flown. Whatever changes were being made must be in the mechanics of it. If Nancy could just find out what the changes were, she might be a lot closer to discovering the leak.

As she reached the end of the road that fronted Jetstream, Nancy yawned. Enough for one night, she thought. A good sleep and she'd be ready to start fresh the next day.

She'd just made the turn onto the road leading back to her aunt's when a pair of headlights glared in her rearview mirror. There was a car behind her, so close that the rear window was blanketed with white light.

Blinded by the light, Nancy tapped the brakes, signaling the other driver to stop tail-gating. The car stayed where it was. Nancy tapped the brakes again, honking her horn to help get the message across.

The car still didn't drop back, but the driver did turn the high beams down.

Enough of this, Nancy thought. She slowed down and edged to the side of the road, hoping the idiot would pass her.

The car behind her merely slowed down, too.

Was someone playing a game? Or was someone following her? There had been other cars on the road when she drove to Jetstream, but she hadn't paid any attention to them. One of them could have followed and waited for her. She decided to find out.

Pressing her foot down, Nancy pushed the Honda to the speed limit. The other car sped up, too. It stayed about a car length behind her and its headlights were on the regular beam now.

With almost no other traffic, Nancy knew it wouldn't take her long to reach the village. The village had lights. If the car stayed with her, she'd be able to get a good look at it. Right then it was nothing but headlights.

The driver must have had the same thought, though. Just before Nancy reached the village, the tail dropped way back.

Okay, Nancy thought. Now we'll find out if this is a game or not. She pulled up at the stop sign, then inched slowly forward. Checking the rearview mirror every second, she wanted to see the other car when it pulled up to the stop sign. At least she'd be able to see what color it was. But the car kept its distance.

Nancy decided to try a new tactic. She gunned the Honda and whipped it around the first corner she came to. Still going as fast as she dared, she turned onto another street, stopped, made a U-turn, and drove back to the corner. She pulled over to the side, parked, and turned off her headlights.

In a second she heard the car screech to a halt. It was at the stop sign.

A few seconds more, and she heard it coming down the street she was facing. It had slowed down, and Nancy knew it had lost her. Now all she had to do was wait.

She didn't have to wait long. In a few seconds a dark car came into view. It was inching along, and as it passed under the outside lights of a bait and tackle shop, Nancy had a perfect view of the driver's face.

The driver was Dmitri Kolchak.

Chapter

Nine

Bess looked out at the empty stretch of beach behind Eloise's property and yawned. "It's only six-thirty in the morning," she said, rubbing her eyes. "There's nobody here but the sea gulls."

"That's the point," Nancy told her. "We can talk without being interrupted."

"We could do that at the house, over cocoa," Bess pointed out. "Hot cocoa," she added with a shiver.

"Come on," George told her. "Run a few minutes and you'll get warm." She and Nancy headed for the wet sand and began an easy jog. Bess tagged along behind, still yawning.

It wasn't long before they all were warm and wide-awake. They slowed to a walk, and Nancy told them what had happened the night before.

"Dmitri Kolchak?" Bess looked horrified. "I can't believe it!"

"I can," George said grimly. "You remember what Nancy said, Bess—he used to be a pilot. That makes him an excellent connection, and his job as chaperon is a great cover."

"I guess so," Bess said reluctantly. "But the plans were stolen a while ago. He wasn't even here then."

"But he could be the brains behind the whole operation, and he's here to get the last of the plans now," George said.

"Why else would he have followed me to Jetstream last night?" Nancy asked.

"Maybe he didn't follow you," George said. "Maybe he was there already, to meet his contact—Bill Fairgate. When he happened to see you, he decided to try to scare you off."

"I thought of that," Nancy said. "Remember the car 'accident' at the beach, Bess?"

Bess nodded. "Of course I remember. I guess it *was* a warning, just like the note you got." Bess thought a minute. "What about Jacques?" she asked. "Do you think he's involved?"

"I don't know," Nancy admitted. "Maybe not. I really don't know anything about Jacques. I don't think I've ever talked to him, except when he was explaining to me about the car. But I'm almost positive about Dmitri." She stopped and used her toes to dig out a shell half buried in the sand. "I should have known it was Dmitri in that car last night even before I saw him," she said. "All that time he had his bright lights on only meant he wasn't familiar with the car.

"And that note on my windshield?" Nancy went on. "Sasha was right about that—there *is* something weird about it. 'Stop now your investigation,'" she quoted. "That *now* is in a funny place. Funny for someone whose first language is English, that is."

"Right," George agreed. "Dmitri's first language is Russian."

Suddenly Bess's eyes widened. "Nancy— maybe he's KGB!" she whispered. "I was joking when I suggested it, but now I think I might be right. He's leaking the plans to the Soviet Union!"

Nancy shook her head. "I don't think so. Jetstream doesn't make military planes or anything. This isn't a breach of national security—it's industrial espionage. And anyway, those plans definitely went to France. It's weird. I wonder how Dmitri got involved as a go-between. You'd think it would be either an American or a French person."

"Don't forget Jacques," George pointed out. "He could be in on it, too."

"You can figure the details out later," Bess

said impatiently. "What are we going to do *now?*"

"I want to follow up on a couple of things," Nancy said. "I need to find out from the car rental place if there really was something wrong with Dmitri's car yesterday. Also, I still need to see the Jetstar plans. Maybe Gary can help figure out a way to get into Jetstream without being turned into dog food."

"I'll talk to him," George said. "He's coming by after breakfast."

"Great." Nancy picked up the shell and juggled it back and forth in her hands. "I wonder," she said. "You don't suppose Marina could be involved in this, too?" She swallowed. "Or even Sasha?"

"I guess it's possible." George said. "Have they done anything suspicious?"

"Not really. Marina's awfully cool to me, but that doesn't mean she's involved in this. And Sasha?" Nancy shook her head, still fingering the seashell. "He's a great guy," she said quietly. "But he's been awfully interested in this case from the start."

"Well, *I* don't believe it," Bess declared firmly. "You might have convinced me about Dmitri, but Sasha? Never!" She patted Nancy on the shoulder. "But don't worry. I'll help you keep an eye on him. I don't have anything else to do, anyway."

Nancy laughed. "What about Yves?"

"Oh, him." Bess shook her head. "I've decided he's not for me."

"Why?" George asked.

"Well, he's gorgeous, and his accent is divine," Bess said. "But he keeps talking about how he'll be retiring soon. Can you imagine? Retiring at age twenty-nine? It makes him seem so old!"

George and Nancy burst out laughing. "You do have a point," Nancy told Bess.

They went back to the house, showered, and made breakfast for themselves. Eloise had gone out already. As Nancy was swallowing the last of her tea, Gary arrived. The lanky pilot looked depressed.

"I just had my interview with Susan Wexler —told her the whole story," he announced. "You don't think she'll break her word and let it run early, do you?"

Wishing she felt as sure as she acted, Nancy shook her head. "Don't worry," she counseled him. "She's looking for a bigger story. She knows she won't get it from us unless she plays fair with us now."

Gary brightened a little. "I hope you're right." Crossing to George, who was loading the dishwasher, he put his arms around her slim waist from behind. "Hey, I know this poor, sad, unemployed pilot who could really use a day out with a pretty girl like you," he said to her teasingly. "Want to meet him?"

George turned to him, smiling and pink cheeked. "That depends," she retorted. "Is he cute?"

"Well, now, I guess he looks kind of like me," Gary told her.

"Let's go," George said promptly. "I have a feeling I'm going to like him!"

"I'll finish loading the dishwasher, George," Bess volunteered. "You two are so cute together it makes me want to cry. Where, oh where, is the man for me?"

"We'll find you one, Bess," Nancy promised as George and Gary left. "As soon as this case is solved."

After she and Bess finished cleaning up and showering, Nancy called the car rental agency at the airport. The man she spoke to was friendly, but not too helpful. They'd never had any other complaints about their cars surging forward uncontrollably, but it wasn't impossible, he told her. The mechanic hadn't found anything wrong with the brakes or timing on Mr. Kolchak's car so far, but those things were difficult to detect. Mr. Kolchak could just have had a heavy foot on the gas pedal. However, it was true that earlier models of this same car had been recalled for exactly the problem Nancy described.

Feeling frustrated, Nancy hung up. That conversation had gotten her nowhere. Glancing at her watch, she saw that it was after eleven. Where had the morning gone?

"Come on," she told Bess. "Let's go to the dance institute and see what our friend Dmitri is up to."

When Nancy and Bess arrived at the institute, they could almost feel the tension as the dancers rehearsed both the new pieces and the traditional ones that everyone knew. The next night was the gala opening, and everyone wanted it to be perfect.

As far as Nancy could tell, Sasha already was perfect. Watching him leap and whirl in time to Yves's music, she couldn't imagine him getting any better.

She tried to tell herself it was only his talent she admired, but she knew it was more than that. Even though she was in love with Ned, something about Sasha made Nancy's heart do somersaults.

"I thought we were supposed to be watching Dmitri," Bess whispered to her after they'd been sitting in the auditorium for fifteen minutes.

"We are." Blushing, Nancy shifted her gaze to the chaperon, who was in the front row, six rows in front of them.

"Nancy," Bess said. "I know you're attracted to Sasha, but that doesn't mean you're going to do anything about it, so stop feeling guilty."

Nancy had to smile. Trust Bess to figure her out. She could spot attractions a mile away.

That's all it is, Nancy told herself. Attraction. And she *wasn't* going to do anything about it. Nodding firmly to herself, she kept her eyes on Dmitri Kolchak.

The Soviet chaperon got up about ten minutes later. A manila envelope tucked under his arm, he strode up the aisle and out of the auditorium.

Nancy stood up the minute the door clanged shut. "George said she and Gary would come by if they found a way to get into Jetstream," she said to Bess. "You stay here in case they do. I want to see where Dmitri's going."

Outside, Nancy saw the chaperon heading on foot toward the main street of the village. Hoping he wouldn't look back, she started after him.

Once he reached the main street, Dmitri walked one block and then stopped in front of a building. Nancy was on the other side of the street by now, under the awning of a bakery. As she watched, Dmitri Kolchak pushed open the door of the post office.

Quickly Nancy crossed the street and walked to the post office. Peering in the front glass door, she saw the chaperon talking to the woman behind the counter. He passed her the envelope, waited while she weighed it, then paid for the postage.

When he came back outside, Nancy was studying a display of fresh seafood in the window of the shop two doors down. Out of the corner of her eye, she saw Dmitri cross the street. When his back was completely to her, she hurried to the post office and went inside.

"Hi," she said to the postal worker. "I was wondering if you could tell me the rates to France."

"First class?" the woman asked.

Nancy nodded. It didn't really matter.

"I shouldn't have to look it up," the woman said, running her finger down a chart. "The man who was in here before you just sent something to France." She glanced up, smiling, to tell Nancy the rate.

But Nancy was already out the door.

Glancing around, Nancy spotted Dmitri halfway down the block. It seemed as if he were heading back to the institute. She would have given anything to see what was in that envelope. If he'd just mailed some Jetstar blueprints to France, there was no way she could prove it. Should she just go up to him and confront him?

Don't be ridiculous, she told herself. He'd just deny it. Plus, if she said anything at all, he'd know she suspected him. Then he'd be even harder to trap.

Dmitri was almost at the end of the road when Nancy saw him go into a food shop. She knew that place—it sold wonderful, thick sandwiches on fresh-baked Italian bread. It was lunchtime; he was probably going to take something back for Marina and Sasha.

Nancy's stomach rumbled. She'd eaten

breakfast hours ago, so she might as well pick up something, too—after Dmitri left.

Waiting outside the little shop, Nancy watched several people come and go. Her stomach was rumbling even louder now, and she wondered what was taking Dmitri so long. Finally, she edged up to the front window and looked inside.

From where she was standing, Nancy could see the cash register. Gathered near it, chatting together, were Dmitri, Bill Fairgate, and Eileen Martin.

Quickly Nancy pulled away and walked back down the block and around the corner. There she waited, peering around the edge of the building.

First Eileen and Bill came out. They got into separate cars and drove off in the same direction. To Jetstream, Nancy guessed.

At last Dmitri stepped out. He carried a bulging paper bag in one hand. Probably sandwiches, Nancy thought. But she was more interested in his other hand. In it was a folded sheet of white paper. He glanced at it, smiled, and tucked it carefully into the pocket of his lightweight windbreaker.

He could have just taken a menu from the sandwich shop, Nancy told herself. Or he could have gotten new plans for the Jetstar—hand delivered by Bill Fairgate.

Chapter

Ten

Giving up on lunch, Nancy started back toward the institute, keeping a safe distance from Dmitri Kolchak.

She wasn't sure what was happening. Had Dmitri actually gone into the Jetstream complex the previous night? Had he gotten something from Bill Fairgate then, and more information at the sandwich shop just now? Then why hadn't he waited and mailed both things at once? If he hadn't gotten anything from Bill the previous night, then what had he just mailed to France?

What about Eileen Martin? She and Bill Fairgate had obviously come to buy their lunch. But with Eileen there, would Bill Fairgate really have dared to hand over secret information?

Nancy didn't have any answers. The paper Dmitri had put in his pocket might have some, though. She had to find a way to look at it.

She also had to find a way to get some leads on Bill Fairgate, Nancy realized. For instance, she could follow up on the reports that he liked to play the stock market. But how could she get any concrete information about his financial status, especially way out here in the Hamptons? If he was playing the stock market, he was probably doing it through a broker in New York. The only thing she could think to do was break into his office, either at work or at home, to look for bank statements or stockbroker's reports. That wouldn't be easy, and Nancy hated to do it if it wasn't absolutely necessary.

As she turned up the path to the institute, Nancy tapped her fingers thoughtfully on her cheek. Maybe she'd come up with a better plan if she just thought about it for a while.

"Well?" Bess whispered, when Nancy slipped back into the seat beside her. "Did he do anything suspicious?"

The rehearsal was still going on, and Dmitri was back in his usual place—front row center, his eyes on Sasha and Marina.

Nancy nodded. "I'll tell you later."

"Okay." Bess rolled her eyes. "It's been crazy here," she said. "Yves threw another fit

90

about his sheet music. I'm really glad I didn't let myself get serious about him." She sighed, and then clapped a hand over her stomach. "I'm absolutely starving. Why don't I go out and get us something to eat?"

As if in answer, Dana Harding suddenly called out, "Okay, lunch, everybody!" Looking at her watch, she added, "We'll start again at one-thirty. Don't stuff; I want you light on your feet when you get back!"

It was twelve-fifteen. Nancy suddenly had an idea. "Let's take Sasha and Marina and Dmitri to the beach for lunch," she said to Bess. "There won't be time to swim, but it'll be a nice break for them from this place. Besides, I still owe Sasha a hot dog."

"I'm tired of hot dogs," Bess remarked.

"Then you can get some fries," Nancy told her, laughing. "Besides, eating isn't the main reason we're going."

"It's not?"

"I'll explain everything to you on the way there," Nancy said. "Come on, let's ask them before Dmitri starts passing out the sandwiches he brought back."

Fifteen minutes later, using two cars, the five of them arrived at the beach. Dmitri hadn't been eager to go, but Sasha talked him into it. Nancy could tell that Sasha was hoping to spend the entire time with her, but if Bess did her part, he was only going to get five minutes.

"Mustard? Sauerkraut?" Nancy asked Sasha

after she'd bought two hot dogs. Bess, Dmitri, and Marina had decided to eat Dmitri's sandwiches.

"The—what do you say?—the works," Sasha told her.

"Relish, too?"

"Of course, relish," he said. "The more stuff, the better." He grinned. "It hides the taste of the frankfurter!"

Laughing, Nancy told the boy behind the counter, and soon Sasha was taking an enormous bite of an overloaded hot dog.

"I hope it doesn't give you indigestion," Nancy said, as they slipped off their shoes and stepped onto the warm sand. "Dana Harding would kill me."

"I can eat anything," he told her, patting his stomach. "This idea of yours was great, coming to the beach," he added. "Look, I think even Marina is glad to be away from rehearsal."

Nancy looked over to where Bess, Dmitri, and Marina were sitting behind a dune, out of the wind. The ballerina was laughing, and even Dmitri was smiling. Bess must have said something funny. Nancy was glad to see that Dmitri had taken off his windbreaker. It was weighted down with his shoes.

Come on, Bess, she said silently. We don't have much time.

As if she'd heard, Bess stood up, casually dusting the sand off her shorts. Still laughing, she glanced far off down the beach. Suddenly she froze. Then she started shrieking, jumping up and down, and waving wildly.

Marina and Dmitri were standing now, too, cupping their hands around their eyes and looking to where Bess was excitedly pointing. She was still shouting, and finally the word *shark* drifted back on the wind.

"Shark!" Sasha cried. "This is something I must see!"

Nancy took his half-eaten hot dog. "Go on," she told him. "I'm not too crazy about sharks, so I think I'll just stay here and eat."

Like a shot, Sasha was off and running, joining the other three as they dashed along the sand.

Nancy grinned to herself. Trust Bess to come up with the most dramatic distraction she could think of. She hoped there was *something* in the water, or Bess would have some fast explaining to do. In the meantime Nancy had to hurry.

She raced over to the dune, put the hot dogs down on a sandwich wrapper, and reached into the pocket of Dmitri's windbreaker. Her fingers closed over a piece of paper, and after glancing around to make sure they were still far away, she pulled the paper out.

In her hand was a program for the next night's dance performance.

Nancy's shoulders slumped. She'd been so sure! Now she felt ridiculous. She should have

known Bill Fairgate wouldn't hand over industrial secrets in the middle of a sandwich shop,
right under the eyes of Eileen Martin.

Eileen was in charge of the programs. She
must have given it to Dmitri when she ran into
him at the shop. All perfectly innocent, Nancy
thought in disappointment.

"Nancy?"

It was Sasha's voice. Quickly she slid the
program back into the jacket pocket and stood
up.

"There you are!" he called, running up to
her. "It wasn't a shark at all. It was just an old,
black air mattress, all torn up. Not by a shark, I
hope," he joked.

Nancy smiled and glanced beyond him. The
other three were coming back, Bess's arms
waving wildly as she talked.

"Nancy," Sasha said. "I can see that you
have something on your mind. It's the
Jetstream case, am I right?" Without waiting
for her answer, he went on, "You said you
didn't want my help. But, Nancy, I have had
many thoughts about it. I truly believe I have
discovered—"

"Sasha, please," Nancy interrupted. "It's
really better if you stay out of it." She wanted
to tell him about Dmitri, but how could she?
She wasn't even sure she could trust Sasha.
"It's true, I've been thinking about the case.
But I can't tell you anything. I wish I could, but
I can't. Please, stay out of it."

Sasha put his hands on her shoulders and looked into her eyes for a long moment. "I won't trouble you with my theories," he said. "But Nancy, promise me one thing."

"What?"

Sasha's blue eyes were serious, his handsome face was full of concern. "Promise me that you will be very careful," he said.

He'd said the same thing, the night before, in the parking lot. Now, why does he keep saying that to me? Nancy wondered. She gazed at Sasha as he picked up his hot dog. Is he just concerned for me? Or does he know something specific?

Just then Bess, Dmitri, and Marina got back and retrieved their sandwiches.

"Bess, I think you must have a remarkable imagination," Marina was saying. "I do not think an air mattress looks anything like a shark." She laughed, her dark eyes sparkling with humor. "It must be fun to be you," she teased.

To Nancy's surprise, Dmitri let out a deep chuckle. "Marina, I do not believe your life can be so bad," he admonished, but he sounded as if he were joking.

Nancy had never seen either of them in so lighthearted a mood. Was it because Dmitri had just mailed the final installment of the Jetstar plans to Aviane? Was Marina in on it, too?

Oh, boy, Nancy realized, I'm really going off

the deep end today. Everyone looks suspicious. Come on, Drew, stick to the facts!

Jumping up, she turned to the others. "Put those sandwiches down," she ordered them. "It's time for a swim. Last one in's a rotten egg."

Nancy raced for the surf, Sasha by her side. She could hear Dmitri huffing along behind her and Bess and Marina giggling.

Nancy decided she should take a break from thinking for a while. Right then, the most important thing to do was to have some fun!

"I can't figure out if Sasha's one of the nicest, most sincere guys I've ever met," Nancy said, "or if he just acts as well as he dances."

She and Bess were back at Eloise's house, fixing dinner. The dancers had taken an early break for dinner and were planning to rehearse late into the night, so Nancy and Bess had decided to leave. George still wasn't back, and Eloise was taking a shower.

"It's awful," Nancy went on, tearing up lettuce for a salad. "I've never had so much trouble figuring somebody out."

"I don't see how you can really believe Sasha is involved," Bess said. She brushed some chicken pieces with soy sauce. "He hasn't done anything strange except ask you about the case. I don't think he'd risk his career over something like this. Besides, he's just too nice."

Nancy smiled. "Plenty of 'nice' people commit crimes, Bess." She measured oil and vinegar into a bottle and shook it hard. "Anyway, even if he's not involved, I can't tell him anything. He might let something slip to Dmitri."

Nancy sighed and stared out the window toward the ocean. "But every time he looks at me with those blue eyes, I want to tell him everything."

Bess glanced at her. "As I said, you're attracted to him."

Reluctantly, Nancy nodded, her eyes still on the ocean. "I hate to admit it, but it's true," she said slowly. "I don't want to believe he's involved in the Jetstream leak either, Bess. But I have to keep telling myself he could be. I can't let the way I feel wreck my investigation."

Bess covered the plate of chicken with waxed paper and walked over to Nancy. "You're worried about Ned, too, aren't you?"

Nancy nodded again. "It's not that I think anything would ever happen between me and Sasha," she said. "I mean, Ned and I have something totally special. I've never really looked twice at any other guy—until now."

Bess started to say something, but the phone interrupted her. She reached for it, said hello, and then held it out to Nancy.

"Talk about timing," she whispered. "It's for you, Nancy. It's Ned."

Chapter

Eleven

SMILING SYMPATHETICALLY, Bess left the kitchen. Nancy's cheeks were hot, and she stared at the receiver for a second, feeling guilty. Finally she cleared her throat and held the phone to her ear.

"Ned, hi!"

"Hi, Nancy." Ned Nickerson's deep voice was warm with affection. "How's the Atlantic Ocean?"

"Wet," Nancy replied, laughing. "Actually, it's beautiful, but I haven't had much time to relax and stare at it lately."

"Why not?"

"It's George's boyfriend, Gary," Nancy said. "Remember, I told you about him?"

"Sure," Ned said. "What's happened?"

As Nancy told him the story, she relaxed a little. It felt good to be talking to Ned. "At first I thought he might actually have done it," she finished. "But he's trying too hard to clear his name."

"Knowing you, I'll bet you've got a pretty good idea of who *is* doing it," Ned told her.

Nancy smiled. Ned always had confidence in her. "I have an idea," she said. "But so far, no real proof." She went on to describe the incidents with Dmitri Kolchak.

"You're kidding!" Ned sounded amazed. "Boy, that would really be something, wouldn't it? I mean, if you caught the chaperon of that dancer you've been showing around. What's his name, Sasha?"

"That's right." Nancy felt her cheeks get warm again. "Sasha Petrov."

"How's he enjoying the Hamptons?" Ned asked. "What's he like?"

"I think he's having a great time." Nancy decided not to answer the second question. "Anyway, that's why we haven't had time to take it easy the last couple of days."

"Too bad," Ned said. "But I know you'll get it all cleared up."

"I hope I do, especially before you come out here."

"That's one of the reasons I called," he said. "I'm not going to make it for a while, I'm afraid. Things are just too busy right now. But don't worry," he added. "I'll show up one of these days."

"I can't wait," Nancy told him, although she couldn't help hoping Sasha would be gone by then.

"Me, either. Okay, I'd better go," Ned said. "And, Nancy?"

"Yes?"

"Be careful."

Sasha had said the same thing, Nancy remembered, feeling guilty again. After she and Ned had said goodbye, she made up her mind to solve this case as fast as she could. Once it was behind her, she could try to figure out exactly how she felt about Sasha Petrov.

Nancy, Bess, and Eloise ate dinner out on the deck and watched the ocean in the distance and smelled the salty air. Low clouds in the western sky were turning pink as the sun started to set.

"The dinner is wonderful," Eloise told them, reaching for a second piece of chicken. "You two can cook for me anytime. I just wish George was here to enjoy it," she added.

Nancy glanced at her watch. "I do, too. I thought she'd be back by now."

"Maybe she and Gary are on to something," Bess said, forking up some salad. "Weren't they going to try to figure out a way to get into Jetstream?"

Eloise looked alarmed. "I hope they don't do anything foolish like sneak in there," she said. "It would look very bad for Gary if they got caught."

Nancy looked down at her plate. She was hoping to sneak into Jetstream herself, but she decided not to tell her aunt. Eloise was really very supportive about Nancy's detective work, but if she knew Nancy's plans, she'd never stop worrying.

"That reminds me," Nancy said, taking another piece of corn. "I found out how Eileen Martin's son died. It would have been terrible no matter how it happened, but a plane crash makes it seem even worse, somehow."

"I know," Eloise agreed. "Eileen doesn't talk about it, not to me, anyway. We're not really friends. But a friend of hers did tell me she was very bitter at first."

"Why?" Nancy asked.

"She blamed the company," Eloise explained. "Something about not checking the plane carefully enough before they let her son take it up."

Bitterness, Nancy thought. It could make people do things they'd never think of doing— just as greed could. "How does Eileen feel about the accident now?" she asked.

"Well, as I said, she hasn't talked about it to me," Eloise told her, wiping her fingers on a napkin. "She certainly seems content enough now."

"It seems that you'd never get over something like that," Bess commented.

Just then they heard the front door slam, and in a moment George and Gary joined them on the deck.

"You're just in time," Eloise said with a smile. "If you'd come any later, I might have finished all the chicken."

The two of them got plates, sat down, and began to eat hungrily. George's eyes were bright with excitement, but she didn't say anything about the case. Bess was right, Nancy thought. They're on to something, but they don't want to worry Aunt Eloise.

By the time the pink clouds had faded to gray, Eloise pushed back her chair and stood up. "You cooked," she said with a smile. "I'll clean up." She stacked the plates and carried them into the kitchen.

When he was sure Eloise couldn't see him, Gary turned to Nancy and gave her a thumbs-up signal. "We're in!"

"How did you do it?" Bess asked, as the four of them drove toward the Jetstream complex later that night. "I mean, you didn't get a key, did you?"

Gary shook his head. "My roommate got the guards' schedule," he explained. "It's posted at the main gate, and the fan belt on his car just 'happened' to break when he drove in this morning."

"The guard let him use the phone at the gate to call the AAA," George said. "He said it took him about ten seconds to copy the schedule."

"Pretty good work." Nancy chuckled. "But what about the dog? I mean, she just roams around, doesn't she? She's not on any schedule."

"And she's mean," Bess said, looking worried. "Nancy said she was real mean."

"Relax." Gary laughed, his hopes high about clearing his name. "Gina's not supposed to roam. What happened with Nancy was the guard's fault. The dog is always supposed to be on a leash."

"Let's hope the guard doesn't make the same mistake tonight," Bess remarked.

Ten minutes later Nancy was parking the car just past the turnoff on the road leading to Jetstream. They set off on foot, all four of them wearing dark clothes, and they used low shrubbery as cover when they passed the main gate. A short time later they'd reached the place at the fence where Nancy had been caught.

Nancy looked across the fence toward the dimly lit door. "You're sure the alarm system's off in the building?" she asked Gary.

He nodded. "It's lucky that it's been broken for a couple of days," he whispered. "That's why they've got two extra guards on tonight, because they won't have the system repaired until tomorrow." Quietly, he unfolded the guards' schedule and looked at it, using a tiny penlight. "We've got exactly eight minutes to get in that door before one of the guards comes to check it."

"Then let's get going," Nancy said.

It took about two minutes for them all to get over the fence. Bess got caught on the top, snagging a leg of her jeans. When she finally broke free, the ripping noise sounded so loud, they all froze, expecting a guard or a dog to be on them in a second. No one came.

"Well," Bess said quietly, "I'm just glad I didn't wear my favorite jeans."

Stifling a laugh, they streaked across the grass toward the door. In seconds they were down in the stairwell. George, Gary, and Bess focused their penlights on the lock, and Nancy went to work with a thin piece of wire.

"Three minutes left," Gary whispered. "How's it going?"

Nancy didn't answer. She'd done this kind of thing a few times, but the wire just wasn't working. It was all she'd been able to find at Eloise's house, and it was too thin.

"Two minutes," Gary said, trying to keep his voice calm. "We're going to hear the guard pretty soon."

Nancy pulled the wire out and tried to bend it. It snapped in her hands.

"Should we forget it?" George asked.

Stuffing the pieces of wire in her jeans

on each drawer," Nancy said,
vith the hair clip. When she got
open, Gary started studying the
me the size of notebook paper,
larger than posters.

!" he said. "They've got the word
ed on them." He kept on searching
blueprints.

o you suppose Bill Fairgate—if he's
did?" George asked. "Take pictures

e," Nancy said. "I guess the informa-
d be sent in some kind of code, too."
e are the latest!" Gary said excitedly,
g to the dates penciled in the corner of
rint. "What did that reporter say?
was talking about the engines?"
ght," Nancy said.

ay, I've got the right ones." Gary
ed them to George, then said, "Now we
engine plans from about two years ago.
l compare the two to see what kind of
nges they've made."

They opened the right file and found the
rresponding blueprints. Then Gary took out
drawing of the entire plane. It was one of the
ig ones.

"Are we finished?" Bess asked anxiously.

"Almost," Nancy said. "But we've got to
make copies. We can't take these originals out.
If anyone ever traced them to Gary, he'd be

---

pocket, Nancy shook her head. She looked up, then narrowed her eyes at Bess.

"What?" Bess asked.

"Your hair clip," Nancy said quietly. "It's not a treasured heirloom, I hope."

Bess already had the clip out of her hair. "It cost all of eighty-nine cents," she said, handing it to Nancy. "Be my guest."

Carefully, Nancy broke the metal part of the clip from the colored, plastic part and worked it into the lock.

"Forty-five seconds," Gary told her.

Ten more seconds passed, and then Nancy smiled. "Got it," she said.

They were in the door with half a minute to spare, but they didn't take time for congratulations. Following Gary, who knew where all the blueprints were stored, they moved quickly and quietly through the dim halls.

"I hope nobody's working late tonight," Bess commented.

"Somebody usually is," Gary told her. "We just have to take the chance and hope we don't get spotted."

At the door of the blueprint room, Nancy went to work again with Bess's hair clip.

"Hold it," George whispered tensely. "I hear something."

"I hear it, too," Bess whispered. "It's footsteps." Her blue eyes were wide with fear. "Somebody *is* working late!"

Chapter
Twelve

NANCY TURNED BACK to the lock, trying to keep her hand steady. "Come on, come on!" she silently urged.

The lock turned at last, and in a tumble the four of them rushed into the room. Nancy stayed by the door, keeping it cracked open in case whoever was walking in the hall was headed for this room.

The footsteps got closer and louder. Nancy held her breath, peering through the hairpin crack.

The footsteps continued on, past the door. Nancy inched it shut and turned to the others.

"It was P...
was carry...
maybe he's
George la...
wasn't taking
Gary was al...
shining his pen...
date? Oh, here. ...
"This isn't the ri...
"Which is the ri...
"I don't know." ...
grim smile. "I'm n...
leaking the stuff, rem...
Nancy was shining ...
drawers. "They use dat...
names," she said. "Just f...
back farther than three ye...
Ten minutes went by, ...
whispered loudly, "This file...
we give it a try? The dat...
recent."
"How's the hair clip holding...
Gary asked.
"I think it'll make it."
Bess laughed quietly. "Not bad ...
nine cents!"
There were three wide, shallow dr...
the file cabinet, with a single lock that...
long rod in place to keep the whole ca...
secure.
"This makes it easier—at least I don't ha...

THE
to pick a lock
and got busy ...
the top drawe...
blueprints, s...
others much
"This is i...
Jetstar prin...
through th...
"What d...
the one—
of them?"
"Mayb...
tion cou...
"Thes...
pointin...
a blue...
Avian...
"Ri...
"O...
hand...
nee...
We...
ch...
co...
a...

through. No one would believe he wasn't the spy."

"We'd be through, too," Bess muttered. "Okay, I see your point. But let's hurry!"

There was a copier in the file room, with extra-large paper in it. Nancy turned it on, praying that it wouldn't make too much noise. It was a fairly new, expensive-looking machine, and it ran with only a faint hum.

Nancy quickly fed the blueprints they'd selected through the copier. Then she switched it off, and they replaced the original prints in the file cabinet. Nancy hoped they'd gotten the right prints into the right drawers—it was hard to be sure, since they all looked so much alike.

When everything was back in its original shape, they divided the copies of the blueprints among themselves, folded them carefully, and tucked them under their shirts.

"There's just one more thing I want to check," Nancy told the others quietly. "Bill Fairgate's office."

"Oh, Nancy, do you have to?" Bess wrung her hands nervously. "I feel like we're tempting fate just by being here."

"I may not get another chance," Nancy explained. "If he's the leak, I need some way of proving it."

Single file, the four friends crept down the darkened hallway until they found Bill

Fairgate's door. Nancy tried the knob. It wasn't locked.

She eased the door open and went in. Gary, George, and Bess stayed out in the hall, waiting anxiously for her.

Nancy shone her penlight around Bill's office. Her eyes widened in surprise. The desk that had been buried under an untidy mound of papers the other day was clean and bare.

Wondering, Nancy pulled open drawer after drawer in the desk. They were all nearly empty, and what was in them was unremarkable: pens, paper clips, rubber bands, neat files of old memos. No bank statements or brokers' reports. No Jetstar blueprints. No notes. In fact, nothing that even remotely resembled current work!

Nancy exhaled slowly. Bill Fairgate was up to something. Maybe he knew someone would be searching his office, and he cleared it out so no one would find anything that might incriminate him. Did that make any sense?

She slipped back out to the hall and reported to the others. They were as puzzled as she.

"Maybe he just cleaned up," George suggested in a doubtful whisper. "Maybe the mess got to him after a while."

Shrugging, Nancy turned toward the exit. "Whatever it is, we can't figure it out tonight," she said. "Shall we go?"

"I thought you'd never ask," Bess murmured gratefully.

"We'll have to be careful going over the fence," Nancy warned.

"Right," Bess agreed. She patted her shirt, and the blueprint underneath it made a rustling noise. "And try not to crinkle too loudly, either."

Quickly and quietly, they moved through the hall to the outside door. Gary checked the guards' schedule, then his watch, and finally nodded to himself. "We're okay," he told the others. "We've got five minutes before somebody checks this door again."

"Mission accomplished," Nancy said. "Let's get out of here!"

It was ten-thirty when Nancy started the car and turned it onto the road leading back to town. "So far, so good," she said to the others. "Just keep your fingers crossed that we'll be able to make some sense out of these blueprints."

"Gary's our expert on that," George said.

"Not quite," Gary retorted, grinning. "But I've taken a few classes in engineering and design—all pilots have to. If we got the right stuff, I think I'll be able to find what we're looking for."

"What exactly *are* we looking for?" Bess asked.

"Some change in the design or engineering —or both," Nancy explained. "If we can figure out what's been changed, then we might be able to tell who's been working on it. That person would have the best chance to copy the changes and pass them on to Aviane."

"Well, from what I saw of these plans," Bess commented, "it's going to be like looking for a needle in a haystack."

"Maybe," Nancy agreed with a smile. "But at least now we've got the haystack."

The farther they got from Jetstream, the more Nancy relaxed. Going in there had been very risky. If Jetstream discovered that the blueprints had been tampered with, Nancy knew there was going to be big trouble. She just hoped they'd find some answers soon. If they did, the risk would have paid off.

Sitting next to Nancy in the front seat, Bess yawned loudly. "I don't know why I'm so sleepy," she said. "I guess breaking into Jetstream is enough to wear anybody out."

"Speaking of getting worn out," George commented, "look—they're still rehearsing at the institute."

Slowing the car down, Nancy glanced over at the dance institute. Bright lights could be seen in the windows of one of the rehearsal rooms.

"That seems kind of cruel," Bess remarked. "The performance is tomorrow night, and Yves told me they'd be rehearsing during the day tomorrow, too. If they don't get some rest, they'll sleepwalk their way through the performance."

"It looks like only a few people are still

there," Nancy said, slowing the car down even more. "I wonder who."

"Uh-oh," Bess said. "I have the feeling we're going to make a quick stop, right, Nan?"

"Right." Passing the institute's parking lot, Nancy pulled the car to the side of the road right at the end of the property. Probably it was just a few dancers, working on a routine, she thought. But what if Dmitri was there? What if he was meeting his Jetstream connection? The institute would be the perfect place for that, she suddenly realized.

"Don't worry, I'll be back in a minute," she said to the others as she got out of the car. "I just want to take a look."

Trotting swiftly across the grass, Nancy reached the main door of the institute. It was unlocked, and she pushed it open, then quietly eased it shut behind her.

Standing in the dimly lit lobby, Nancy could hear the sound of voices coming from the rehearsal room down the hall to the left. There was no music, and she didn't hear any sounds of bodies leaping or moving. She knew the dancers could just be discussing a routine.

Moving on tiptoe, Nancy left the carpeted lobby and turned down the hall toward the rehearsal room. It was the only one with lights on; all the other rooms were dark.

One person was speaking now—a man— and his voice became louder as Nancy got closer. Halfway down the hall, she stopped, her heart pounding. The voice was speaking in Russian, and it was the voice of Dmitri Kolchak.

Swallowing hard, Nancy moved forward again. The door to the rehearsal room was halfway open, and light spilled out into the hallway. Nancy crept up behind the door and peered through the crack.

Dmitri was still talking, but she couldn't see him. The only person she could see was Marina. The dancer wasn't in her rehearsal clothes; she was wearing jeans and a pink cotton pullover, and her hair was a mass of tangles, as if she'd just gotten out of bed.

Just then, Dmitri crossed Nancy's line of vision. She didn't get a good look at his face, but he sounded angry, and before he moved out of her sight, he pounded a fist into the palm of his other hand.

The chaperon wasn't talking to Marina, and Nancy knew there must be a third person in the room.

Dmitri's voice softened, then got loud again. Nancy couldn't understand anything he was saying.

Finally Dmitri stopped talking. Nancy held her breath, keeping her eyes on Marina. The ballerina turned her head and said something to the third person.

Finally, the third person spoke. Nancy had no trouble recognizing his voice. It was Sasha Petrov.

Still out of Nancy's sight, Sasha spoke quickly and forcefully in Russian. Nancy closed her eyes, frustrated at not being able to understand him.

At last, though, Sasha said something she *did* understand. It was only one word, but the word was *Jetstream*.

Chapter

Thirteen

BEFORE NANCY HAD TIME to think about what she'd just heard, Marina interrupted Sasha. Looking back and forth between the two men, who were still invisible to Nancy, the ballerina spoke quickly and angrily, tapping at the watch on her slender wrist.

She wants to go, Nancy thought. And I better go, too, before they spot me.

Nancy wanted to run, but she was afraid of making noise. Forcing herself to move slowly, she backed down the hall, keeping her eyes on the door. If she saw a shadow cross it, she planned to slip into one of the other rooms. No one came, though, and Nancy could still hear their voices as she reached the end of the hall.

Once she got out of the building, Nancy gave in to her urge to run and was back at the car in seconds.

"What happened?" Bess asked as Nancy slid breathlessly into the driver's seat. "You look really upset!"

Nancy started the car and drove off. On the way home, she told her friends what she'd heard. "So it looks like all the Soviets are in it together. I guess I shouldn't be upset, but I am. I'm disappointed, too." She shook her head and shrugged. "Anyway, let's not talk about it now," she said, pulling up in front of Eloise's house. "Let's get to work and see if we can find that needle in the haystack."

The house was quiet when they let themselves in. "Aunt Eloise must be asleep," Nancy whispered. "Let's try not to wake her. The less she knows about what we did tonight, the better."

Quietly the four of them tiptoed into the kitchen. Bess started a pot of coffee, and George found a box of doughnuts in the bread drawer and put them on a plate.

Nancy helped Gary spread out the blueprints, and then they all gathered around the kitchen table.

Bess's eyes widened as she looked down at the intricate drawings. "Where on earth do we begin?"

Gary grinned at her. "At the beginning."

An hour and two cups of coffee later, Gary shook his head and whistled.

"What?" George asked. "Did you find something?"

"No." Gary shook his head again. "I hate to admit it, but this is a lot more complicated than I thought. But don't worry," he added. "Something'll show up."

"Look," Bess said, using her doughnut as a pointer. "The engines are at the back. That's kind of different, isn't it?"

"Yeah, but they didn't build it with the engines in front first and then rebuild it with them at the back," Gary said. "It's always been that way." He held up the two-year-old blueprint and tapped it with a finger. "See?"

"What's the point of putting them on the back?" Nancy asked.

"Less resistance," Gary said. "When they're in front, they pull the plane. In back, they push it. That's kind of a simple way to put it, but basically, that's it."

"The simpler the better," Bess remarked. "But does it change the way they're built or wired or something if they're at the back?"

Gary looked thoughtful, then snapped his fingers. "Maybe it does in the Jetstar, Bess," he said happily, "you might just have hit on something there." Reaching for another doughnut, he bent over the table again.

But Gary's excitement proved premature.

Bess had given them an idea, but even with that, they couldn't seem to find any earthshaking change in the blueprints.

Another hour later George straightened and rubbed a crick in her back. "It's got to be here!" she said in frustration. "Unless Aviane was just lying to Susan Wexler."

"They might have been," Nancy agreed. "I hate to say this—maybe we just didn't find the right blueprints. Or the latest ones."

"You mean Bill Fairgate—or whoever—has them?" Bess asked.

Nancy nodded. "He was carrying a briefcase when he left. Maybe he took them home with him tonight," she suggested.

"But he'd have to leave the originals at Jetstream, wouldn't he?" George protested.

"I would have thought so," Nancy said, rubbing her eyes. They felt as if they were full of sand. "I guess he could return them in the morning, as long as he made sure no one saw him."

Gary looked worried. "He did clear out his office. Maybe he's getting ready to leave the country and take the final plans to Aviane in person."

"We can check on it tomorrow, but I doubt he'd risk that," Nancy said, shaking her head. "He'd know there's no way he could get out of the country once Jetstream discovered he was the spy—which they'd figure out pretty fast if he didn't show up for work one morning. And anyway, if it became provable that Aviane had been mixed up in industrial spying, Jetstream would slap them with a lawsuit that would break them. The only way they can possibly get away with what they're doing is by covering their tracks completely."

Nancy looked at the clock over the stove. It was two-thirty in the morning. The doughnuts were long gone, and nobody could stand to look at another cup of coffee.

"Listen," she said, "we're all wiped out. I don't know about the rest of you, but I'm having trouble seeing straight. Let's call it off for tonight. Maybe we'll be able to find something after we get some sleep."

Everyone agreed, but they were all disappointed. They'd known it wouldn't be easy, but they thought they would solve it.

After Gary left the three girls took the blueprints up to their room and hid them in the closet.

"Has anybody thought about how we're going to find out if Bill Fairgate has the latest blueprints?" George asked, peeling off her jeans.

"I can't think of anything but sleep," Bess said, yawning widely. Then she looked at Nancy, who was standing at the sliding doors leading to the deck. "Nan?" she asked. "You're still upset about Sasha, aren't you?"

Nancy finished tying the belt on her short yellow robe and turned around. "I'm more upset about not solving this case tonight," she said. "But you're right, I'm upset about Sasha, too."

"You heard only one word," Bess pointed out. "It doesn't prove anything."

"Bess is right," George agreed, pulling on the big T-shirt she slept in. "I mean, they found that blueprint in Gary's locker, and everybody but us believes he took it. So just because Sasha said something about Jetstream doesn't mean he's involved in the spying."

"I know." Nancy shook her head, annoyed with herself. "Here I am, worrying about Sasha, when it's Gary who's in trouble." She stepped into her flip-flops and headed for the door. "I'm going to take a shower. Maybe that'll clear my head."

The warm shower felt great, but Nancy's head wasn't any clearer when she got out.

Bess and George were right, she told herself as she toweled herself off. She couldn't decide Sasha was guilty without proof. Still, it didn't look good. She was almost positive Dmitri was involved. So why else were Sasha and Marina having a midnight meeting and talking about Jetstream if they weren't involved, too?

What made it really bad was the attraction she felt for Sasha. If only she couldn't stand him!

Suddenly Nancy felt so tired she couldn't think straight, about anything. Her eyes burned, and every time she closed them, she saw blueprints. Her hair was still damp, but she didn't care. She brushed her teeth and went back to the guest room.

George and Bess were already asleep in the twin beds. The three of them took turns, and it was Nancy's night for the futon. She unrolled it and stretched out, planning to listen to the low roar of the ocean for a few minutes. But she was asleep the minute she closed her eyes.

When Nancy woke up, she could tell by the light that it was late. Sitting up, she rubbed her eyes and looked at the clock on the dresser. Almost ten.

Nancy rolled up the futon, dressed quickly in a pair of white cotton shorts and a blue tank top, and headed for the kitchen. George and Bess were already there, and so was her aunt Eloise.

"Hi," Bess said when Nancy came in. "How'd you sleep? I had nightmares about blueprints all night."

"Don't worry," George said, when Nancy looked guiltily at her aunt. "We told her what we did."

"I should have known something was up when you left here dressed like cat burglars last night," Eloise said, pouring a glass of juice for Nancy. "I can't say I approve, but I certainly understand. I'm just thankful you didn't get caught."

"I am, too," Nancy said, sipping some juice.

"Now we've got to figure out where to go from here. I wonder if Bill Fairgate is in today? I think I'll make an appointment to talk to him if he's there."

"Call Jetstream and ask," George said. "Also, how about taking another look at those blueprints? Now that we've had some sleep, maybe we can spot something. I think I'll call Gary," she added, "and see if he's awake yet."

The phone rang as George started for it. Eloise was closer and picked it up.

Nancy was putting bread in the toaster when Eloise, still on the phone, cried, "Oh, no!"

Nancy glanced over at her aunt. Eloise looked shocked, and she was gripping the phone tightly. "You're sure?" Eloise asked. "That's horrible! What could— Please, try to calm down. I know it's awful, but you can't afford to get hysterical."

Nancy, George, and Bess exchanged puzzled glances.

Eloise listened intently, getting paler by the second. Finally she said goodbye and hung up.

"Aunt Eloise?" Nancy said. "What happened?"

"That was Dana Harding." Eloise cleared her throat. "This is simply unbelievable— Sasha Petrov is missing!"

Chapter

Fourteen

"MISSING!" BESS CRIED. "What does she mean? How could he be missing?"

"Dana is absolutely beside herself, so I'm afraid she couldn't give me many details," Eloise said. She took a deep breath and let it out slowly. "All she managed to tell me was that Sasha didn't show up for rehearsal this morning. Neither Dmitri nor Marina knows where he is."

Forgetting about her toast and the plans she'd been making, Nancy headed for the door. "Come on," she said over her shoulder to Bess and George. "Let's get over to the institute and find out what's going on."

"Call me!" Eloise cried out as the three girls raced to the front door.

"I will!" Nancy shouted back. "Try not to worry!"

Nancy tried not to worry herself, but her hands gripped the steering wheel nervously as she drove. What could have happened between last night and this morning? What had Sasha done? If his disappearance was connected to the Jetstream case, then why hadn't Marina and Dmitri left, too? Or was Sasha on his own?

Nancy pulled the car up in front of the institute, braking sharply, and the three girls ran into the building.

The lobby and the auditorium were buzzing with people. Many of the dancers were wandering around in confusion, trying to find out what was happening. Others were standing in little knots, talking worriedly. A few members of the institute's board were there, including Eileen Martin. She was holding a stack of programs and talking to Dana Harding.

Dana was wringing her hands and acting completely beside herself, as Eloise had said. When Dana saw Nancy, she left Eileen and came running over, her eyes frantic with worry.

"Eloise told you?" Dana asked.

Nancy nodded. "When did you find out Sasha was missing?"

"Just a little after nine," Dana said, "when Dmitri and Marina came looking for him here.

The last time they had seen him was last night, around eleven-thirty, they said. They were all going to bed then, or so they thought. They have no idea what time he left the house after that. Dmitri was up at seven this morning, he says, so it could have been any time between midnight and then."

Around eleven-thirty, Nancy thought. Not long after she had seen them in the rehearsal room. What could have happened after that?

"I just don't know what to do!" Dana cried, running a hand through her hair. "I know Sasha likes to have fun, but I don't think he'd play this kind of joke. What if something awful's happened? Maybe I should cancel the performance tonight! Good heavens, how can I worry about the performance when Sasha could be in danger? Oh, I don't know what to do!" she said again.

Nancy put a hand on her shoulder. "Try to calm down," she said. "And don't do anything about the performance yet. Have you called the police?"

"Yes. I waited as long as I could, hoping he'd turn up." Dana took a shaky breath. "They should be here any minute."

"Where are Dmitri and Marina?"

Dana looked around distractedly. "They were here just a minute ago," she said. "Maybe they went into the auditorium. I *hope* that's where they went. If Marina's disappeared, too, I'll lose my mind!"

Nancy patted her shoulder and went into the auditorium. Bess and George were there, talking to some of the dancers. Nancy spotted the two Soviet dancers standing by the piano on the stage and started toward them.

She was halfway down the aisle when Dmitri saw her. Even in the dim light, Nancy could see that he was furious.

"You!" he said, as she came up to them. "I hold you fully responsible for this!"

His reaction was the last one Nancy had expected. Completely surprised, she just stared at him.

Dmitri started to go on, but Marina interrupted. "It was your mystery," she said to Nancy. "The case you are trying to solve. Sasha could talk about nothing else."

"Yes!" Dmitri agreed, his voice harsh with worry. "And to think I actually indulged him by driving him to that airplane factory that night, just so he could see what you were doing!"

Nancy finally found her voice. "Sasha was with you that night?"

Dmitri looked embarrassed. "So, you *did* see me. I was afraid of that," he said. "Yes, Sasha was with me. But he was hiding in the back seat, out of sight."

Nancy just shook her head, not quite understanding.

Dmitri sighed. "Sasha had this crazy idea of solving the mystery with you," he explained.

"If only you hadn't encouraged him!" Marina cried.

"Encourage him?" Nancy said, climbing onto the stage. "I didn't encourage him, Marina. I told him just what Dmitri did—that he was here to dance, not to solve mysteries."

Marina's dark eyes widened. "But your case —it was all he talked about to us!"

"To me, too," Nancy told her. "But I didn't ask him to help me with it. I told him to forget it."

Dmitri collapsed onto a folding chair. "Then we owe you an apology, Miss Drew."

"I owe you one, too." Nancy took a deep breath. "You see, I decided you were involved in this Jetstream case."

"What?" Dmitri cried incredulously.

Nancy told them about how she had begun to suspect Dmitri after he followed her that night, and about how she had trailed *him* to the post office the day he mailed something to France.

"France?" Dmitri blinked in bewilderment. "I merely sent our hosts there a copy of our itinerary. We go to Paris from here, you know."

"I know," Nancy told him. "But Aviane is a French company, and you'd already been acting so suspiciously— Well, anyway, I suspected you of sending industrial secrets," she concluded with a wry smile. "And last night just about convinced me."

"Last night?" The chaperon frowned. "What do you mean?"

Might as well tell him everything, Nancy thought. Maybe it'll help find Sasha. "I saw the three of you here last night," she explained. "I couldn't understand what you were saying, but I did hear the word *Jetstream*. And I thought you were . . ." Her voice trailed off.

"Plotting something?" Exchanging glances with Marina, Dmitri almost smiled. "No," he said. "I heard Sasha going out the door. It was late, and I couldn't understand where he might be going at that hour. Marina heard *me*, and together we followed Sasha over here. He was looking for evidence, he said."

"He said he had learned something," Marina told Nancy. "He was very excited, because he was sure it would help you break the case."

"Did he tell you what the evidence was?" Nancy asked.

"We didn't even ask," Marina said. "We just tried to convince him to stop."

Nancy sat down on the piano bench, thinking hard. Could Sasha really have stumbled across something?

As if he'd read her mind, Dmitri said, "Miss Drew, if Sasha *did* learn something, then it's possible his disappearance is connected to this case."

"You could be right," Nancy agreed grimly. "What happened after you talked to him here?"

"We all went back to our house," Marina said. "Sasha said he was going to bed, but he must have sneaked out again." She stopped, looking frightened. "If you and Dmitri are right, then he could be in danger!"

Nancy had already thought of that, but she didn't want to worry them any more by agreeing. "Listen," she said, "I think you should go back to your house and check his room. He might have left some kind of message or clue about where he went."

Dmitri appeared to be glad to have something to do besides stand around and worry. He walked up the aisle, and Marina followed him, but first she turned to Nancy.

"Please, Nancy, forgive me for being so cool to you before," she said. "Sasha was very attracted to you from the first, and I was afraid he would get so distracted he would neglect his dancing."

"It's all right," Nancy said with a smile. "But I don't think you have to worry about his dancing. He's great."

"Yes," Marina agreed. "But he and I are very different. He gets interested in so many other things. And I truly thought you were encouraging him with this detective business." She bit her lip nervously. "Do you think you will be able to find him?"

"I'll do everything I can," Nancy promised. With a shaky smile, Marina thanked her, then continued up the aisle.

After she'd gone, Nancy put her chin in her hands and leaned her elbows on the piano keys. The noisy crash of notes made Yves Goulard stick his head in the door, but Nancy decided to ignore him. She wasn't hurting anything, and this was a good place to think. After a second the accompanist threw her a black look and withdrew. Staring blindly at the sheet music, Nancy tried to figure things out.

Talk about jumping to conclusions, she thought, furious with herself. She'd been so sure about Dmitri. It turned out he'd just been going along with Sasha, trying to keep him from getting into trouble.

That trip to the post office had meant nothing at all. The "secret meeting" between Dmitri and Bill Fairgate at the sandwich shop was completely innocent. The car accident really was an accident. And now Nancy was back where she'd started—in the dark.

Or was she? There was still that note she'd found on her car. She was sure the writer's first language wasn't English. Then, Sasha claimed he was on to something. He'd come here last night, to the institute, to try to find out more.

There had to be a connection between Jetstream and someone at the institute. But who? Could it be Jacques? It might not be fair to suspect him just because he was from France, but she had to start someplace.

Looking around, Nancy realized that she was alone in the auditorium. Bess and George and the other dancers had left. The police were probably there by now, she thought. She'd talk to them, and then try to find Jacques.

As Nancy got up, she bumped the piano, sending the sheet music sliding to the floor. Down on her knees, she started to gather it up, hoping Yves wouldn't notice and throw another fit. One of the sheets had drifted under the bench. She reached for it and picked it up. Then she froze.

Nancy hadn't seen this particular piece of paper before, but she'd spent most of the night looking at ones like it.

She was holding a copy of a blueprint from Jetstream.

Chapter

Fifteen

Yves Goulard. Of course, Nancy thought, her hand gripping the blueprint tightly. The temperamental accompanist who freaks out when anyone goes near his music. The twenty-nine-year-old who's already making plans to retire. The Frenchman who speaks English beautifully but probably doesn't write it as well, especially in a threatening note. Yves Goulard had to be the current link between Jetstream and Aviane.

Hearing voices from the lobby, Nancy suddenly realized how exposed she was. Yves could come back in here any second. In fact, he was probably waiting until the piano was clear.

With all the turmoil, he must not have been able to get to the blueprint yet. The last thing Nancy wanted was for him to find out she knew.

Her hands shaking, Nancy quickly but carefully slid the blueprint in with the rest of the sheet music and set it all back on the piano. Then she jumped off the stage, hurried up the aisle, and went into the lobby.

The first person she saw was Yves, standing with Dana Harding. The minute he saw Nancy, he frowned, checked his watch, and started toward the auditorium door.

Nancy actually held the door for him, giving him an innocent, helpful smile as he passed. Then she let out her breath and went over to George and Bess, who were standing with some dancers.

"Come on!" she said urgently, motioning them to follow her outside. She didn't say another word until they'd reached her car. Then she told them everything.

"I can't believe it!" Bess cried, her cheeks flaming in anger. "I mean, I believe it, but it's still incredible. No wonder he's ready to retire—he must be making a mint!"

"Any clue about who his contact is at Jetstream?" George asked. "Can we connect him to Bill Fairgate in any way?"

Nancy shook her head. "Not yet. I'm more worried about Sasha right now," she said. "Yves has to know where he is. Dmitri told me that Sasha was looking for something over here last night. The argument I overheard in Russian was Dmitri and Marina trying to talk Sasha out of trying to solve this case."

"You mean he was working on his own?" Bess asked.

"Right. And he must have stumbled on something," Nancy said. "Anyway, Sasha left with Dmitri and Marina. But then he went out again. Somehow, Yves must have figured out that Sasha was on to him. I don't know if Sasha called and told him or asked to meet him or what, but I'm sure Yves knows where he is."

"What are we going to do?" George asked. "Stick with Yves and hope he leads us to Sasha?"

"No, I want to search Yves's house." Nancy turned to Bess. "Do you know where he's staying?"

Bess nodded. "He told me. He's got a little cottage by himself, the last place on Dune Road. No wonder he never invited me there," she added, still angry. "The place is probably crammed full of blueprints."

Nancy couldn't help smiling. "Don't worry, Bess, we'll get him. In the meantime, you stay here and keep an eye on Yves while George and I go out to his house. If he looks like he's getting ready to leave, call. Let the phone ring twice, then hang up. Do you have his number?"

Bess nodded again. "I sure do. The creep!"

This time Nancy laughed. Then she and George got into her car and drove toward Yves's cottage on Dune Road. Nancy wasn't sure what they'd find. All she could do was hope that Sasha was all right.

Dune Road didn't have too many houses on it. In spite of its name, it wasn't on the dunes—it was a few streets in from the ocean. The houses on it were smaller and less luxurious looking than many others Nancy had seen in the Hamptons.

"It looks empty," George said, as she and Nancy walked the last few feet toward Yves's cottage. They'd left the car partway down the road and come the rest of the way on foot. If anyone else was there, they didn't want the sound of the engine to give them away.

"There aren't any cars around," Nancy agreed. "But I guess there's only one way to be sure." Taking a deep breath, she reached out and knocked on the front door. She waited, slowly counted to ten, then knocked again, harder.

"Well?" George asked.

Nancy tried the door. Locked. "Too bad I threw away Bess's hair clip," she commented. "Come on, let's see what's around back."

At the back was a small flagstone patio, and sliding glass doors leading into the house. The glass doors were covered on the inside with a big bamboo shade.

136

"We're in luck," Nancy said, testing the doors. "This one's almost off its track. I guess Yves's not much of a handyman."

The door was enough out of line so that by pushing and sliding at the same time, Nancy was able to move it about half an inch along the track. That was enough for her to work her fingers into the opening and lift up the lock.

It didn't take long, but it made a lot of noise. When she slid the door open, the whole thing shrieked and rattled so loudly, they were afraid the glass would break.

"I guess if anybody else *is* here, they've heard us by now," George remarked.

"Right," Nancy agreed. "So what have we got to lose? Let's go in."

Pushing the bamboo shade away, they stepped into a small, neat kitchen. A door opened into the living room, and they could see part of a baby grand piano in there.

Nancy and George stood still for a moment, listening for sounds. The house was quiet and felt empty. Cautiously, they moved into the living room.

"What exactly are we looking for?" George whispered.

"Anything to do with Jetstream," Nancy whispered back. "But mostly anything that might lead us to Sasha."

Nerves on edge, they walked around the living room. Nancy stopped at the piano, but she didn't really expect to find anything. Yves wouldn't bother to hide blueprints in the sheet music in his own house.

George spotted a canvas carryall near the front door and looked questioningly at Nancy.

"Might as well," Nancy said.

Unzipping the carryall, George began to rummage through it.

The phone and a notepad were on a low table next to the couch, and Nancy walked over to it. Maybe she'd get lucky and find a phone number scribbled on the pad.

"Just swimming stuff," George muttered, zipping the carryall back up. "And lots of sand."

The notepad was empty. Nancy pulled open the little drawer in the table, and a couple of pencils rolled around noisily. Still nervous, Nancy reached in and stopped them.

The house was silent again. Then Nancy thought she heard something. Her hand still on the pencils, she raised her head and listened. "I heard it, too," George whispered, her dark eyes wide. "It came from upstairs."

Both girls held their breath and listened. There it was again. A thump, coming from directly over their heads.

Nancy put her finger to her lips, tiptoed to the bottom of the stairs, and looked up. The landing was empty.

Leaving George downstairs as the lookout, Nancy slowly climbed the stairs. There were two doors on either side of the small landing.

One was half open, and Nancy could see a chest of drawers and part of a bed. She stuck her head all the way in. The room was empty.

The other door was closed. Just as Nancy put her hand on the knob, she heard the thump again. She turned the knob quietly and inched the door open. Then she flung it wide.

In the middle of the room, gagged and tied to a straight-backed chair, was Sasha Petrov.

In seconds Nancy was at his side, undoing the cotton kitchen towel tied around his mouth.

"Nancy!" Sasha gasped when the towel slipped off. "How did you know where to find me?"

"I didn't," Nancy said, working on the knots at his wrists. She was so relieved at finding him safe, her hands were shaking. "I found out about Yves, though," she explained, "and I was hoping something in this house would lead me to you."

His hands free, Sasha quickly untied his ankles and stood up, shaking his arms and legs to get the circulation going. Then he turned to Nancy and hugged her, quickly and hard. "Thank you," he said quietly.

"You're welcome." Nancy hugged him back. Then she stepped away and took his hand. "Come on. George is probably going crazy downstairs. You have a lot of explaining to do, Sasha Petrov," she added with a grin, "but it can wait until we're out of here."

George bit back a cry of surprise when Sasha came down the stairs. Grinning irrepressibly, Sasha threw her a cocky salute. Nancy rolled her eyes, astonished at him. Didn't he realize how much danger he'd been in?

"Let's hurry," she said, shepherding George and Sasha out the door before either of them could start talking. "We should get back before Yves starts wondering where I went. He looked at me pretty hard after he saw me sitting at his piano. I'm sure he's asking himself what I saw."

"I overheard Yves on the phone," Sasha told them, as they drove back to town. "It was the night before last, at the institute. I didn't know who he was talking to, but I heard him say 'Jetstream' a couple of times. And he was very edgy."

"So you put two and two together?" George asked.

"Of course!" Sasha proclaimed triumphantly. "Isn't that what detective work is all about, Nancy?"

"Sure," Nancy said, her eyes on the road. "But it's not about putting yourself in danger, at least, not if you can help it." She glanced over at him. She was still relieved, but she was beginning to feel annoyed, too. "What did you do? Call Yves and ask to meet him or something?"

Sasha nodded. "It was stupid, I agree. After Marina and Dmitri and I went back home last night, I called Yves. He suggested I come to his house so we could discuss things. I walked part of the way, and then he picked me up and drove me the rest of it."

"And?" George asked. "What did he do, knock you out? I can't believe you walked into that one."

"I didn't," Sasha protested, but he didn't sound terribly insulted by George's comment. "I was prepared for him to attack me. Don't forget, I am a dancer. I have very quick reflexes. Also, I have a little training in the martial arts.

"However, Yves didn't have to fight me." Sasha twisted around and smiled at George. "He had a gun, so I decided to do exactly as he said."

"*That* was smart, at least," Nancy remarked.

"I refuse to be insulted," Sasha said cheerfully. "And you will stop being disgusted with me once you hear this—Yves made a call from his house last night. I was upstairs, but he hadn't shut the door." He paused dramatically, his blue eyes sparkling with excitement. "There is going to be another Jetstream delivery. Tonight," he added. "Right before the performance."

"No kidding!" George cried. "You're sure?"

"As sure as possible," Sasha said. "I wasn't able to tell who he was talking to, unfortunately. But I could tell he wasn't happy. He kept saying he had to have them both this morning.

But the person couldn't do it, I guess. Finally, Yves said, 'All right, all right. Tonight, before curtain. Same place. And be careful.'"

"'Same place,'" George said. "It must be the piano."

Sasha turned to Nancy, smiling. "Well, Detective. What do you think?"

Nancy couldn't help smiling back at him. "Tonight," she said, "I think we're going to set a trap. And it should be quite a performance!"

Chapter

Sixteen

By SEVEN O'CLOCK that night, an hour before the dance institute's opening performance, the trap was set.

From Yves's house, Nancy and George had driven Sasha to Eloise's. There, Nancy had made several phone calls. One was to the police. One was to Gary, to let him know he was almost in the clear. Another was to Dmitri, telling him Sasha was safe. Finally she called Susan Wexler, the reporter. "There'll be a big story tonight," she told her. "And it isn't about the ballet."

After that, Nancy went back to the institute

and told Bess and Dana Harding what had happened. Dana was horrified, but she had agreed to keep Yves busy the rest of the day working with Sasha's understudy. That way, Yves would have no chance to go home and discover that Sasha was free. Sasha himself was going to sneak into the institute about half an hour before curtain time.

Now, at seven o'clock, Nancy was standing backstage with Bess and George. They'd been helping with costumes and backdrops, but finally they'd stopped, too edgy to do anything but wait.

"If it doesn't happen soon," Bess said, "I think I'm going to scream."

"I know how you feel," George told her. "I just wish it was over."

"It will be soon," Nancy said. Keeping her fingers crossed that nothing would go wrong, she looked around the backstage area. The piano was downstage right, just behind the curtain. After the first two dances, it would be rolled off, and the orchestra would take over. Yves had placed his music on the piano only a few minutes ago, and then had gone back to one of the dressing rooms to change into his formal clothes.

Four police officers were in the auditorium —two backstage and two at the exits. Nancy knew who they were, but she was sure no one else could tell. The two backstage were wearing jeans and T-shirts and had been working on the lights. The other two were dressed as ushers.

Dana had managed to find a substitute pianist, a thin young man named Russell, since Yves wouldn't be playing if all went as planned. She had fretted that Russell wouldn't play the cues the same way Yves did, but Nancy comforted her somewhat by suggesting that she make notes on Russell's copies of the sheet music so that Yves's replacement would know what to do.

Now Russell was hovering nervously by the edge of the stage, studying the cues and tapping out chords on his knee. Then Dana appeared and whisked him away for a final run-through in one of the practice rooms.

Another twenty minutes went by, and the girls could hear people starting to file into the auditorium. "We'd better go," Nancy said. "We're the only ones standing around doing nothing, and it looks weird."

She was right—the backstage area was a madhouse, with dancers warming up, technicians moving backdrops and working on lights, and several members of the Cultural Society milling around. The noise on the other side of the curtain was getting louder, too— the auditorium was filling up.

"Okay," Bess agreed. "But I'm not going very far. I don't want to miss this!" She and

George went over to talk to Eloise, and Nancy picked up a piece of rope someone had left in the middle of the stage.

She was winding it up and looking for someplace to put it when she saw Yves Goulard walking toward his piano. Dark-haired and handsome in a formal black suit, the accompanist sat down on the bench and reached for the music. He shuffled through it, put it back, and then sat quietly. There were fifteen minutes left until the performance.

Nancy stood still, the rope in her hands. It's going to happen soon, she thought. She glanced around, making sure the police officers were watching. They were, and so were Bess, George, and Aunt Eloise, who'd been told everything. Nancy could almost feel the tension in the air, and she was afraid Goulard might feel it, too, and suspect something. But it was a gala night, she reminded herself. Tension was normal.

A sudden burst of movement caught Nancy's attention, and she looked away from Yves Goulard to see what had happened. A group of dancers had run onto the stage and started warming up. Nancy could tell they were nervous and jittery. They probably don't need to warm up, she thought. They just need to blow off some steam.

Only about fifteen seconds had passed, but when Nancy turned her eyes back to the piano, everything had changed. Yves Goulard was still there, but he wasn't alone anymore. Someone was standing next to him, quietly chatting with him.

As Nancy watched, every muscle tense, Eileen Martin reached out a hand toward the sheet music and slipped a sheet of paper in between its pages.

The police officers closed in then, and the trap was sprung.

The gala was a tremendous success. Yves and Eileen had gone quietly, once they saw that they were surrounded. The whole arrest had taken place behind the curtain, so no one in the audience would even know it had happened until they read Susan Wexler's scoop in the paper the next morning. A few of them may have wondered what sudden illness had made Yves Goulard miss his opening night, but Russell did so well that no one could have thought about it much.

As the orchestra played the opening strains of Sasha and Marina's pas de deux, Nancy settled back in her seat with a sense of anticipation. She knew how hard they'd worked the last few days. Now she would see how the work had paid off.

Sasha soared into his grand jeté, and Nancy heard the other audience members gasp. *He looks like he's defying gravity,* she thought with a prickle of wonder. In everyday life he's great enough—but on stage he's magical!

The music crescendoed. Nancy felt a sharp pain in her arm. Startled, she looked down and saw that Bess was pinching her. "You're staring like an idiot!" Bess told her in a loud whisper. "I think you have a problem. You're really falling for Sasha!"

Nancy shushed her friend and turned back to the stage, but she felt a blush mounting in her cheeks. Could Bess be right? Could she be falling for the Soviet dancer?

The question continued to plague her once the performance was over and the reception had begun. When Nancy spotted a familiar head of golden brown hair and a pair of bright blue eyes coming toward her, she suddenly felt overwhelmed. She couldn't face Sasha right then. Murmuring an excuse, she fled the party and drove home alone.

"I was totally shocked," Bess said. "I mean, Eileen Martin, of all people!"

It was the next morning. The three girls and Eloise were having a late breakfast on the deck off the kitchen.

"She was so nice and friendly," Bess went on, reaching for a slice of melon. "After all that stuff you said about Bill Fairgate, I really expected it to be him."

"I was surprised, too," Nancy admitted,

"and I shouldn't have been. I saw her at the institute yesterday morning, delivering programs. That's when she must have delivered the next-to-last blueprint, too, but I never suspected." She took a roll and began buttering it. "But Eileen had a strong motive."

"You mean revenge?" George asked. "Getting back at Jetstream because of what happened to her son?"

Nancy nodded. "She must not have stopped feeling bitter about it, or stopped blaming Jetstream, even though she pretended to. She told the police that Aviane contacted her two years ago, and she held out for a while, but finally she gave in. Yves was the latest contact they had sent her."

Eloise shook her head sadly. "Well, at least it's over now," she said, "and things can get back to normal. What about Gary?" she asked George. "He must be so relieved."

"He is," George agreed. "He called just a little while ago, from Jetstream. Jetstream apologized and actually offered him a raise."

"Great!" Bess said.

"What about the Jetstar?" Eloise asked.

"Gary told me we were on the right track," George said. "But we didn't have the latest blueprints because Eileen had them. It *was* some kind of tricky wiring, because of where the engines were. You had the right idea, Bess."

"It was Nancy's idea to get those blue-prints," Bess said. "And after the other night, I don't care if I never see another one."

"I'm with you," Nancy agreed. "It was worth it, though, since everything worked out for Gary."

"It sure was," George said. "We're going to spend the afternoon playing volleyball at the beach to celebrate."

"Volleyball?" Bess shook her head. "What kind of celebration is that?"

"That's just this afternoon," George said, grinning. "Tonight, we're going out for a candlelight dinner for two."

"Now that's more like it!" Bess said approvingly.

Not long after that, Gary came by for George. Bess had another crush—this time on one of the Canadian dancers—and the two of them went off bicycling together. Eloise had a meeting with the Cultural Society, and after she left, Nancy was alone in the house.

Feeling restless, she decided to go for a walk on the beach. She pulled a loose white top over her green swimsuit and was almost at the back door when the front doorbell rang. Spinning around, Nancy walked through the house and opened it. She felt a strange little fluttering in her stomach. Sasha Petrov was standing there.

"Nancy! Good morning." Sasha was wearing a bathing suit himself and a T-shirt that matched his sparkling blue eyes.

"Sasha, hi," Nancy said. She glanced past him and saw Dmitri pulling away in his rented car. The chaperon gave her a friendly wave as he drove off. "Where's Dmitri going?"

"Oh, errands, I think," Sasha said with a grin. "Actually, I persuaded him to drop me off here. I wanted to invite you for a walk on the beach."

"That's just where I was going."

"You see?" Sasha said as they headed toward the dunes. "We think alike."

Nancy laughed. "It was just a coincidence."

"Oh, no, it wasn't," he protested. "After all, didn't we think alike on this case? Admit it, Nancy, I would make a pretty good detective."

"Okay, okay," Nancy said, feeling her worries slip away. He was so charming! "You helped me solve it, and I'm really grateful. Of course," she added teasingly, "a really good detective wouldn't have let himself get kidnapped."

"True." Sasha waved his hand as if getting kidnapped were a minor problem. "Next time, I will be more careful."

"Next time?" Nancy stopped walking and looked at him. "You're not serious, are you? I mean, you were spectacular last night, Sasha. The whole performance was great, but you were special. You really wouldn't give up dancing, would you?"

He threw back his head and laughed. "Of course not," he told me. "I know I was meant to dance. But if a mystery comes along now and then, I will not ignore it, that's for sure."

Walking to the water's edge, Nancy and Sasha let the waves roll up over their feet and ankles. Then they walked along the wet sand, looking for shells. The beach was beginning to come alive and the air was filled with salt spray and the smell of suntan lotion.

Suddenly Sasha stopped walking. "Nancy," he said, and his eyes were serious. "I want to say how grateful I am to you for finding me yesterday."

"You don't have to thank me," Nancy said. "Really, Sasha. I'm just glad you're all right."

"I will admit, now that it is over, that I was very frightened."

Nancy nodded. "I was, too."

"Nancy." Sasha put his hands on her shoulders. "I know you asked me to back off, because of Ned. And I have, haven't I?"

Nancy nodded again. She felt his fingers tighten, but she couldn't make herself pull away.

"But, Nancy," he went on, "I don't want to back off anymore. I will, if you insist. But you must tell me again."

Nancy was quiet. How could she tell him to back off when she wasn't sure she wanted him to?

As if he could read her mind, Sasha pulled her closer, leaned down and gently brushed her lips with his. Then he stood back, smiling at her.

Nancy suddenly realized that she was smiling, too. She had no idea what things would be like the next day, or a week from then. But right that minute, everything felt wonderful.

Next in the Summer of Love Trilogy:

Nancy's summer in the chic Hamptons beach resort is growing hotter by the day. She's seeing more of Sasha Petrov, and she's not sure if it's friendship or if it's love. Meanwhile, the new guy in Bess's life, waterskiing instructor Tommy Gray, has drawn Nancy into a mystery of a more sinister nature.

Tommy's mother owns an art gallery, and a painting by one of her artists, Christopher Scott, has vanished. Scott's nephew died only a few days before in a suspicious accident, and now the artist himself is nowhere to be found. Was it murder? And if so, who was the victim? . . . Find out in *PORTRAIT IN CRIME*, Case #49 in the Nancy Drew Files™.